T0157059

O My Beloved

O My Beloved

F, PRASHENJIT SHOME

PARTRIDGE

A Penguin Company

Copyright © 2013 by F, Prashenjit Shome.

ISBN: Softcover   978-1-4828-0078-4
             Ebook   978-1-4828-0077-7

All rights reserved. No part of this book may be used or reproduced by any means, graphic, electronic, or mechanical, including photocopying, recording, taping or by any information storage retrieval system without the written permission of the publisher except in the case of brief quotations embodied in critical articles and reviews.

Because of the dynamic nature of the Internet, any web addresses or links contained in this book may have changed since publication and may no longer be valid. The views expressed in this work are solely those of the author and do not necessarily reflect the views of the publisher, and the publisher hereby disclaims any responsibility for them.

Printed in India.

Partridge books may be ordered through booksellers or by contacting:

Partridge India
Penguin Books India Pvt.Ltd
11, Community Centre, Panchsheel Park, New Delhi 110017
India
www.partridgepublishing.com
Phone: 000.800.10062.62

CONTENTS

"When two hearts are in love then life becomes more promising and brighter then ever before." Anopam said. "Life is full of dreams, promises and lots of plans for the future. True love exist on the heart if there is honesty and trust."

"You poor man, you are really unfortunate. You were affluent of only alcohol. In the long twenty years of my married life you had squeezed out all the tear of my eyes. Today not a single drop is left in my eyes to mourn your death. You poor man, you are really unfortunate." Anuksha said silently.

— ONE —

"Finding out loved one is like finding the most precious thing of life." Anuksha slowly laid her head on the warmth of Anupam's loving arms and she felt the heavenly warmth was never before. She felt very comfortable and secured in his arms and slowly shut her eyes.

"My heart and soul was crying for long years to unite with you." Anuksha said still shutting her eyes. "I was so unfortunate for long years but today I think I am the happiest woman in the world."

Anupam looked down at Anuksha with sort of fascination. He softly caught her hand." Illusive time has altered but you haven't." He said smiling with a light stroke on the tip of the nose. Anuksha smiled a naughty smile and then she was greatly delighted as he kissed her head.

Anuksha felt that she was twenty years young girl once again on the loving arms of Anupam. She felt her skin was growing young and glowing like a twenty years young girl once again.

"We are in love once again newly." Anuksha whispered softly biting Anupam's lobe with a smile.

"You are very naughty". Anupam squeezed her nose.

No one was there only they were two together. The bright sun of merry love was shinning around them. There was no sorrow no pain only fragrance of love and joy.

"I have found my man I love most from my heart and soul." Anuksha said in a pleased voice. "You are the most lovable man who understands me."

Instinctively Anuksha drew herself to him "I love you, Anupam, I love you." She said in excitement. She looked at his face with such a rare expression, only a woman has such expression to a man she loves most.

Anupam looked at her with sort of fascination again. "I love you too." He whispered and kissed her almost wildly.

"I haven't anyone to love but only you." Anuksha said. "Love me, Anupam, love me." She suddenly cried out hugging him like a hungry girl for love. "Spare me in the joy of your love, relief my aching heart and soul from pain of long years."

"Of course I love you." Anupam said with a tinge of joy. "It looks so funny. You are a love-sick woman" He smiled squeezing her soft cheek gently.

Anupam bent over her face and kissed her face twice very affectionately and the sweet waves of kiss travelled through her whole body, she was thrilled.

Anupam put his arms around Anuksha and drew her close. He held her tightly but very affectionately.

He went on wildly and affectionately. She was starving for true love and for the clasp of loving arms for long years. She was fulfilled today.

Anuksha lay on the bed beside Anupam thinking the past years of her life, thinking how she spent the awful years. Of course past life was a dark period of her life. Her past was a tragedy. Her past life was a tragedy from childhood. Suddenly she became nostalgic thinking the past years of her life. Her mind flew back to the beginning.

– TWO –

Life is awful without mother for a child and it was true in the case of little Anuksha. Bad days began in little Anuksha's life from the day her mother died. Everything went wrong into her life after her mother's death. Gradually as she grew up she could feel that her father doesn't love her. Every now and then he abused her without any reason as if she was not his daughter

Gradually Anuksha became prey to her father's abusiveness and her beautiful life was made hell. Her father was an irresponsible, drunkard and abusive person. He always lived in his own world of alcohol. He didn't show any fatherly love and care to Anuksha. He never allowed her to go to the school when other girls went to the school. Rather he told her to do work at home. He always came drunk at night and scolded her without any reason.

As Anuksha grew up she came to know that her father didn't like her mother also like her. He always quarreled with her. Sometimes their quarrel turned to be violent. Anuksha's father made her mother's life a hell.

In the three years of her marriage life, her mother was never happy even for a day. Anuksha's father always troubled her mother physically and mentally as if he found some kind of psychological pleasure torturing her. She was living a life of hell and suffering till the last day of life.

Anuksha's father destroyed all the dolls, vases and other articles made by her mother. He didn't want to keep them at home. He didn't want to keep any memory of her. Because he thought those things would bring bad luck to him and they will remind him about her and he didn't like that.

Anuksha's father Arindom Dutt was a demon looking man with big eyes and big moustache. Pox marks on the face made his look so ugly. He hardly talked with Anuksha and most of the time he was speechless at home. She was afraid of him very much. She had no respect to her father rather she had a kind of fear to her father.

Anuksha's father never took care of little Anuksha. She grew up without care and love of her father. Her father forced her to do some works which she didn't like.

Anuksha's father never asked her likes and dislikes. What she likes to eat or what she likes to wear. Whatever she was given by her father she accepted without any protest.

One day in the morning father took Anuksha to the market. After shopping father told her to carry the bag though she couldn't, though it was too heavy to her age as if it was her punishment for doing any wrong.

Day after day and night after night went on the same thing. There was no one to whom she might turn. There was terror in her thought.

Anuksha hated the life her father forced to lead. She lay awake on the bed with tears in eyes and pressed the brain to find out some way to escape from it but somehow she had no courage or where to go she didn't know.

By then one day a distant relative Neena aunt came as if she had come to rescue her from the hell. She called Anuksha near her. She affectionately held Anuksha and ran her fingers softly on her head.

"You know, Anuksha." Neena aunt said hugging her lovingly.

"Your father has no one to look after him except you. So you should love your father."

Anuksha slowly nodded her head; "I can realize that as a daughter." Anuksha said, "But when I see him angry and drunk than truly I am terrified."

"Don't say like this." Neena aunt said. "After all he is your father."

"Okay." Anuksha said.

Neena aunt loved Anuksha like daughter. She took her into her arms. She softly kissed on her forehead and hugged her for a long time in silence. Tears silently ran down her face. It was really an emotional moment between them.

"Would you like to go with me?" Neena aunt asked looking into her face.

"Yes." Anuksha quickly answered shaking her head. A pleasant smile crossed her face. "Please take me with you. I don't like to stay here. I always feel here very lonely and insecured though I have a father with me."

"Don't worry; I will take you with me." Neena aunt said. "I will tell your father about this."

"Really you are my good aunt." Anuksha said pleasantly hugging her.

— THREE —

Neena aunt appeared in Anuksha's life as a little glow of hope.She took Anuksha to her home at Darjeeling though her father opposed. He didn't like the idea of sending her daughter to Neena aunt's home. Neena aunt got her admission in the same school where she worked as a teacher.

Neena aunt was most popular and respected mistres in the school. Everyone loved her very much for her kind nature and she also taught the students whole-heartedly.

Anuksha could breathe some fresh and free air after long years. She felt the taste of freedom. She was glad and happy she was never before.

Anuksha met plenty of beautiful girls there. She had a great time there. She played along with all the girls and they shared their happiness and joy among one another.

Neena aunt bought her new cloths, cosmetics and new books on different topics and also whatever Anuksha wanted Neena aunt gave her. She never refused. She was passing her days there very happily.

Then two years later with sudden one noon Anuksha's father arrived Neena aunt's home to take her back to Calcutta.

"I have missed you for two long years, my child. Anuksha's father said. "I have come to take you back home. I feel very lonely at home without you."

"I don't want to go back home." Anuksha said in tearful eyes. "I want to stay with Neena aunty. She loves me very much. I am happy here."

Anuksha's father looked at her with a rare kind of expression in his eyes. "You are like your mother." He mumbled.

Anuksha was silent standing against the wall. There were still tears in her eyes. She bowed her head down as if she didn't want to look at her father.

Anuksha's father stared at her. "What are you thinking my child?" He asked. His voice was affectionate. I have employed a new maid especially for you. She is a good cook also. She can cook so many dishes. She will cook new dishes for you every day."

But his sweet words couldn't change her mind. She was still silent bowing her head down.

Neena aunt appeared there. She told Anuksha's father that he shouldn't take her back home. She is well there. She is getting good education there.

"Okay my child." Anuksha's father said with a long sigh looking at her. "If you think you are happy here then I don't force you to go back home with me. Take care of you. Good bye." He lit a cigarette and left.

After that it was nearly six years before Anuksha saw her father again. Even he neither wrote any letter to her nor phoned to her. He only occasionally sent her pocket money by mail.

Anuksha was very good and sincere in her study. So every teacher loved her too much. Among all her school principal Mr. Hariharan took extra care of her. She respected him. For her he was the only wise man in the world. He had vast knowledge and he always wanted to share his knowledge among all. "Knowledge is not anyone's personal property." He said. "Knowedge should not be caged. Knowedge should be distributed among all for the progress of the society."

Mr. Hariharan always said that Anuksha was the jewel of the school. She had brought great honour to his school.

Mr. Hariharan was a tall and handsome gentle man with gold-rimmed glasses. He had two sons but he couldn't make them educated. That was his biggest upset of life.

When Mr. Hariharan praised Anuksha then her heart filled with joy. Sometimes he took her for long walk. He always walked in his casual style putting his two hands crossed and slightly leaning his head forward. He discussed so many topics with her from politics to movie.

— FOUR —

-Every child deserves the pure love of mother. During the holidays when other girls visited their homes then Anuksha preferred to stay at Neena aunt's home because she had no mother. There was no one to love her at home. Sometimes these feelings brought tears to her eyes.

By the way holiday time was great time for Anuksha, which she always loved. During holidays she traveled different places with Neena aunt. Neena aunt was also a very travel crazy woman. Traveling was her hobby. More you travel more you gather knowledge. Travel is a source of knowedge. She always said.

Neena aunt knew to cook different delicious dishes. Italian dishes were her favorite. She often cooked Italian dishes and fed her.

The housemaid of Neena aunt had a great love for Anuksha. She was good dancer too. When Neena aunt was out of home then she showed her dancing skills to Anuksha and made her almost strange. She was amazed.

"Why don't you try to perform on the stage?" Anuksha asked the housemaid.

"That is not written in my destiny." The housemaid answered. "I am destined to be a housemaid not a famous dancer." She laughed. There was hidden pain of heart in her laugh.

Neena aunt bought a new house and they shifted to the new house. It was a small but a wonderful house on the top of the hillock with a beautiful garden in the front. The windows were facing towards the roads and snow covered Himalaya was seen distinctly.

Anuksha always sat on the small wooden bench in the garden after school and looked at the people walked past the garden in the afternoon. She exchanged talk with some of them known to her. It gave her great joy and fun.

When Anuksha was at class eight then Neena aunt arranged a home tutor for her. His name was Anupam Dutta. He was a science graduate and searching for a government job. Basically he taught her science and mathematics.

Anupam was a brilliant student of a reputed college of Calcutta.

Anupam was a young handsome boy of twenty two. His nose was sharp, eyes were wide and round. Among all his polite behaviour was most attractive.

Anupam had a beautiful style of teaching. Whatever he taught Anuksha she could catch very easily.

After that Anuksha's result improved better than ever before. She always got the highest marks in Science and Mathematics. Neena aunt was very much happy in the improving result of Anuksha. She told her to do more hard work for better result. But Anuksha gave full credit to Anupam for her improving result. "Without his help I couldn't do such a good result." She said.

Days went on. Slowly Anuksha developed a soft corner for Anupam in her heart though he was many years older than her.

One afternoon Anupam took her to the hillside. There was a small river coming down the hill to the valley.

They sat by the river stretching out their legs. They picked up small stones and threw into the water. The small stones went down producing small sounds and that gave them wonderful joy.

Anupam looked at her. She also looked at him. They wanted to talk to each other so many things. They wanted to express their feelings of minds but they couldn't. They were silent.It is called love. That can't be explained. That can be felt only.

A few moments later Anupam broke the silence.He threw a fascinating gaze at her.

"Have you ever come to the hillside before?" Anupam asked softly. He softly touched her hand pulled towards him.

"Never," Anuksha answered with a shy look.

"I often come here when my mind is upset." Anupam said. "First I came here when I was five years old. Look at the surrounding scenery.It is too marvellous and romantic.The snowy peak of the mountain Everest is looking at us as if blessing us! Really it delights the mind and mesmerizes eyes."

Anupam held Anuksha's hand and went down the hill to a small fisherman's colony where fishing nets were hanging around everywhere in the outside of the small cottages. Some fisherwomen were pouring different kind of fishes on the ground from the bamboo made baskets.

"These fishermen supply fishes to the different parts of the state." Anupam said. "You know dry fishes contain high protein. It is a good source of protein."

"I know." Anuksha shook her hand slowly. She put her handkerchief into the nose to prevent the smell of dry fishes.

"I like the smell very much." Anupam laughed. He made a little fun with her.

Anuksha had a smile on her lips.

Anupam took a Chocolate out of his pocket. "This is for you." He said, holding out the Chocolate to her.

"Thanks." Anuksha said. "She took the Chocolate from his hand. She removed the wrapper and broke the Chocolate into two pieces and held out one piece to Anupam.

"No it is for you." Anupam said. "Please don't give me"

"If you don't eat then I will be upset" Anuksha said. "Please you take one piece then I can digest it."

"Okay." Anupam said and took one piece from her hand. "I don't want to hurt you. Hurting you means I am hurting myself".

They were walking down the small lane chewing chocolate and afterglows kissed them from the sky.

Anuksha slowly turned her look at Anupam. "Actually where do you belong?" She asked.

"Actually I belong to Calcutta." Anupam answered.

"Calcutta?" Anuksha said almost excitedly. "I also belong to Calcutta."

"I know." Anupam said "Where in Calcutta?" He asked.

"Jadavpur," Anuksha answered quickly.

"My home is very near to Jadavpur." Anupam said.

"Where do you stay here?" Anuksha asked.

"I stay here at my maternal uncle's home." Anupam said. "Who is a government officer at Agriculture department? Actually I am staying here for a government job. My maternal uncle had assured me to get a job in his department."

"Now-a-days it is very difficult to find a government job." Anuksha said.

"Yes, of course." Anupam said. "Let see what is written in my luck."

Anupam looked at Anuksha with a sort of fascination.

"How did you know Neena Aunty?" Anupam asked.

"Neena aunt is a distant relative of my father." Anuksha answered. "She had been unmarried forever so she loves children very much. She loves me like her daughter. After death of my mother there was no one to look after me. Though I have father but he is a drunkard. He does not love me. He doesn't think that he had responsibility towards me so Neena aunt had brought me here."

"Truly Neena aunt is a very kind woman." Anupam said.

"I also think myself enough lucky to have such a kind aunt." Anuksha said. "Truly I have no word to explain."

It was a quiet and beautiful afternoon. September breeze brought some sweet coolness to their bodies. An unknown thrill touched them from inside, they felt but couldn't express.

"What is your full name?" Anuksha asked as they crossed the road.

"Anupam Choudhury." Anupam answered in a soft tone.

Anuksha had a look at Anupam." Your name has quite similarity with my name" she said. "It is amazing."

"Yes." Anupam said smiling. "Both of our names start with the alphabet A."

They burst out laughing.

— FIVE —

When two hearts are in love then life becomes too promising and brighter then ever before. The life becomes full of dreams, promises and lots of plan for the future.They also had lots of dream and promise for the future.

The rest of the year Anuksha spent at Neena aunty's home was wonderful. She passed the days joyfully. She was never bored even for a moment.

Every moment Anupam's shadow surrounded her. Every moment she spent with him was so wonderful and joyful. She was so excited when Anupam put an arm around her and walked down the calm and quite path of the hill through the green bushes.

Anupam was the first man in her life. Before him she never had a boy friend. For her it was a beautiful creation of god for her.Anupam lived in her thought, her dream.

Anuksha loved everything Anupam said to her. They often went out for long walk down the road. She talked everything with him without fear and hesitation.Even she talked about future plan.

Anupam could recite poetry very nicely. He won so many prizes in the recitation competitions. When he recites Keat's poems then it was so wonderful to hear and she was fascinated.

Though there was a vast difference between their ages yet they were same from their hearts and souls.

Anupam called her "little heart" and she loved the name.He loved her innocent and beautiful smile too much.He said I always desire to see your beautiful smile.It makes my mind so fresh.

When Anuksha was sad then Anupam delighted her with ludicorous jokes and she was forced to laugh. They played like two kids throwing pillows at each other when they were alone.

"What is the meaning of true love? Do you know little heart?' Anupam asked throwing a soft and smiling look at her.

"No," Anuksha answered in a blushing gesture.

Anupam put an arm around her shoulder smiling. "True love is immortal" He said." Love brings two hearts and souls together. True love exists in the heart if there is honesty and faithfulness."

Those summer days were so wonderful. She ran after Anupam. He hid into the thick bushes of the park and she tried to find out him. When she couldn't find out her after long search then she almost cried out like a kid and he hurriedly came out from the bushes and hugged her affectionately and she quickly buried her face into the warmth of his bosom and felt a wonderful feeling that she had no word to explain.

Anupam held her hand and walked down the road.

"I have nothing to give you except love." Anupam said looking at her with sort of affection.

Anuksha was silent for a moment then she slowly turned her soft eyes at him. I don't want anything from you." She said. "You have love for me and you have given me shelter in your heart that is enough."

"I don't have knowdge about love. I only know that it can't be explained." Anupam said throwing an arm around her and pulling her close to his body.

Suddenly Anuksha pressed her head against Anupam. "I don't know anything but I love you from my heart." She whispered like a child. "My heart can feel the restlessness of your heart."

"There is always fascination in love." Anupam said smiling. "Love is like a tender bed where two lovers sleep together and dream of a beautiful and joyful future."

Truly those were the days, full of joy in her life. During those happy days one-day abruptly the sad news shattered her soft heart forever. The news was just like a nightmare for her. That was beyond her imagination.

One morning Anupam came and told her that he had got a job in Kuwait and within a week he will leave for Kuwait. She had felt that someone has put a heavy rock on her heart. She couldn't stop her tears. She burst into tears.

Anupam took her into his arms. He consoled her. He looked into her eyes. She wept like a kid silently. He wiped her tears lovingly from eyes.

"Please don't go away leaving me alone. "Anuksha said with tearful eyes. "Please don't go." She grasped him tightly.

"I am not going to Kuwait forever." Anupam said calmly. "I will come back very soon and till then you have to wait. You continue your study heedfully."

Anuksha's tears didn't seem to stop. Tears rolled down her face silently. Her eyes were swollen.

"Don't be silly my little heart." Anupam whispered. "A beautiful life is waiting before you. Now you give more concentration into your study. Your examination is very near. I want a better result from you. I will be back very soon." He mildly kissed her.

As Anupam proceeded towards the door she held his hand from back.He slowly turned to her. She looked at him in tearfull eyes. "When I am going to meet you again? She asked sorrowfully.

"Very soon" Anupam said. He gave a soft kiss on her head and left.

That day Anuksha's tears didn't seem to stop. She wept for hours. Continuous weeping had swollen her eyes.

Anuksha felt she is deserted, she is a lovelorn. She felt very lonely. For many weeks her sleep was violently disturbed. Nothing could pacify her. All the time she remembered him. She thought he would come back but didn't.

Neena aunt looked at Anuksha's swollen eyes.

"What is the matter, Anuksha?" Neena aunt asked, "Any problem with you? Don't hide anything from me."

Anuksha couldn't give any answer. She only muttered indistinctly something and turned her look away as if nothing had happened to her.

One morning Anuksha walked through a small by lane across Anupam's maternal uncle's home with burden of sorrow.

Anuksha pressed the calling bell. Anupam's maternal aunt opened the door and came out. She threw a soft glance at her.

"You are Anuksha?" Anupam's maternal aunt asked with a smile. "Am I right?"

"Yes." Anuksha shook her head with a fade smile.

Anupam's maternal aunt took her inside into the drawing room and offered a chair.

"Anupam always talked about you." Anupam's maternal aunt said. "He always told that Anuksha is very nice girl. She is very brilliant."

Anuksha was silent for a while. Then she glanced up at Anupam's maternal aunt with great curiosity. And what he talked about me?" She asked excitely.

"Many more" Anupam's maternal aunt said with a sweet smile. "He left a letter for you. But I had forgotten to send it to you."

Anupam's maternal aunt got out of the chair and went inside and came back to the drawing room with the letter and gave it to the hand of Anuksha.

Anuksha took the letter from Anupam's maternal aunt with great excitement.

"You read this letter." Anupam's maternal aunt said. "I am going to the kitchen to make coffee for you.

"Okay." Anuksha said calmly.

Anuksha was more excited as she started to open the letter.

"My little heart,

Forgive me. I have left you alone in the kingdom of our memories.I am also carrying your sweet memories in my heart to remember you all the time so that I can feel your presence beside me. I love you.

"Yours Anupam"

Tears almost rushed out of her eyes as she started to read the letter with great interest.

Anuksha finished reading the letter until Anupam's maternal aunt came back to the drawing room with two cups of coffee and some biscuits on a tray. Anuksha quickly wiped her tears off with the back of her hand and tried to be easy as if nothing had happened to her.

Anupam's maternal aunt sat beside Anuksha on a chair. Anupam's maternal aunt gave a mild sip into her coffee. Then she slowly turned her eyes at Anuksha.

"Anupam was a very nice boy." Anupam's maternal aunt said. "He was very brilliant also. He had a good academic career. But his luck was very bad. He could not find a good job here. So he had to leave for Kuwait for a job." She slowly adjusted her glasses. "His heart was very soft." She said. "He couldn't tolerate other's sufferings. He was always ready to help a needy."

Anuksha was listenning everything silently sipping her coffee.

"Let's go to Anupam's room." Anupam's maternal aunt said.

Anupam's maternal aunt took Anuksha to Anupam's room. As Anuksha entered into Anupam's room joy filled her heart. She suddenly felt his presence everywhere around the room.

Anuksha sat down on the bed where Anupam slept. It was a nicely designed bed. She softly touched the bed cover that gave her a wonderful feeling.

A small-framed photograph of Anupam was placed on the table. Anuksha had a long look at the photograph. She got out of the bed and walked over to the table. She pulled the drawer and saw a passport photograph of Anupam inside the drawer. She looked around and hurriedly took out the photograph and put into her frock.

— SIX —

Anuksha's final year result of twelve classes was out. She passed the examination in first division. Then one afternoon suddenly her father appeared at Neena aunt's home without any information to take her back home. This time he was adamant to take her back home along with him.

Anuksha was very sad to leave Neena aunt's home. She didn't want to go back home to live with her father. Fear brought tears to her eyes. Neena aunt was also very much worried about Anuksha's father's decision to take her back home. She was afraid of thinking Anuksha's uncertain future.

Anuksha went to the school to meet her friends and teachers for the last time. It was a painful moment for everyone. Tears came out of everyone's eyes.

"I will miss you." Anuksha said in tearful eyes.

Neena aunt couldn't stop her emotion. Tears rushed out of her eyes. She embraced her affectionately.

"You will write to me." Neena aunt said. "At least one letter every month whenever you want you will come to my home. My door is always open for you. By the way you will look after your father. He is growing old now. But don't forget to take your own care."

Anuksha was ready to leave Neena aunt home. A taxi was waiting in the outside to take her to the bus stand.

Neena aunt escorted Anuksha over to the taxi. Her all luggage were loaded into the dickey of the taxi. As Anuksha's father opened the door and got into the back seat, she followed him and closed the door in her side.

Neena aunt was waving her hand and the taxi disappeared at the far end of the zigzag road.

It was afternoon when they reached home. At home Anuksha was greeted by the new housemaid.

Anuksha had seen a vast change both in the outside and inside of the house even the surrounding area. Six years before she went to Darjeeling there was a huge empty plot beside their house where all the children of the colony played in the evening but now the whole plot was occupied by a huge tall building and so many families from outside the colony had settled there. Over the six years pollution had increased due to increase of vehicles in the road.

The house had not been painted for many years. The walls looked faded. In many parts, the wall was eaten by the dampness.

When Anuksha went into her father's room then smell of alcohol almost suffocated her. The room looked deserted. Everywhere there were only wine bottles and corks on the floor. The floor was dirty and broken. Thick layer of dirt covered the marbles and her father's clothes were carelessly hanging from the hangers on the wall.

"Anuksha," Father said. "Don't come to my room. I know you don't like it."

By then the housemaid entered into the room. "This is my daughter." Anuksha's father said to housemaid.

"She is very cute." The housemaid said smiling.

The housemaid followed Anuksha into her room. The room was clean and fresh. New curtains were hanging in the windows. A new bed sheet was spread over the old quilt of the wooden bed. The clock was still on the same place on the table. The brass vase she bought from a fun fair was still shining on the corner of the room.

Anuksha stood in front of the mirror and looked at her image into the mirror.

The housemaid looked at Anuksha with greater curiosity.

"So your name is Anuksha?" The housemaid asked. "How old are you?"

"I am seventeen." Anuksha answered swiftly.

"But you look much younger than your age." The housemaid said. "Your face is so pretty." She softly touched Anuksha's cheek.

Anuksha blushed.

"Your room was very dirty." The housemaid said. "It was closed and unused for long time. I told your father many times to open the room but your father never listened to me. Then that day one week ago he opened the room and told me to clean the room properly. Perhaps he had thought that you would be angry if you see the room dirty."

"Actually my father had been always careless about the home and his family." Anuksha said.

The housemaid had a glance at Anuksha. "As I entered into your room dirty odour stuck into my nose." The housemaid said. "I was about to vomit. The whole room was covered with thick layer of dust and there were cobwebs in every corner of the room. I did so hard work to clean the room."

"Lot of thanks to you," Anuksha said with a very pleasant smile in her face.

"I can't change your father." The housemaid said. "He doesn't listen to me. All the time he is busy with his wine."

"No one can change my father." Anuksha said.

"I have complained lots about your father to you." The housemaid smiled. "Now you change your dress and get fresh with cold water. I am going to make meal for you. By the way do you like noodles?" She asked as she turned to leave the room.

"Yes." Anuksha shook her head. "Noodles are my favourite."

Anuksha closed the door. She quickly changed her dress then she went to the bathroom and washed her face with cold splash of water. She touched the cold water of home after so many years. She had a great feeling.

Anuksha opened the windows. Air struck into the curtains and afternoon light entered into the room.

The housemaid brought tea and noodles into the room. After drinking tea and eating noodles Anuksha went out of the room and looked around for father.

But father was not at home. He had already gone out of home.

About half an hour later Anuksha's father entered into the house with a bottle of whisky in hand. He directly walked into the kitchen. He took a glass from the shelf and went to his room and closed the door from inside.

After finishing his wine Anuksha's father opened the door of his room and came out. He was little unstable. His eyes were red. He came near Anuksha. He placed a hand over her shoulder. "Krishna is a very good housemaid." He said, "If you need anything then tell her. She is a good cook too. She can cook delicious dishes. She will cook delicious dishes for you."

Smell of wine came from father's mouth. Anuksha couldn't tolerate the smell. She pressed her nose with the fingers. She was burning in anger.

"You are my lovely daughter." Anuksha's father said. "I will take you to the market tomorrow for shopping. I will buy you some new dresses."

Anuksha was pleased to hear. "Okay." She nodded her head slowly.

Anuksha threw a soft look at her father. He had lost his past strength. He had lost his weight. There was no blood in his veins. There was only alcohol in his veins. Alcohol had eaten him before age.

Anuksha noticed a vast change in his father's behaviour towards her. He showed sympathy towards her. But yet she had a doubt whether it was acting or real.

Anuksha adorned her room beautifully according her own way. She kept everything properly in proper places. The housemaid visited her room many times and helped her.

"That yellow dress is beautiful." The housemaid said pointing at the dress at the hanger. "Where did you buy it?" she asked.

"I bought it from a market in Darjeeling." Anuksha answered.

"Your choice is wonderful." The housemaid said.

It was nine O'clock at night. The housemaid set supper at the dining table. She went to Anuksha's room.

"Supper is ready." The housemaid said. "Come to the dining table. Now you are tired and hungry. Don't wait for your father. He is always late to come."

Anuksha finished her supper and went to the bed. She was lying on the bed with a magazine in hands. Slowly her eyes were heavy with sleep. She put down the magazine in one side of the bed and slowly raised her head up and looked at the clock. It was about five minutes to eleven O'clock. Then a few seconds later she heard father's voice. He was almost drunk. He passed by her room mumbling something indistinctively.

Then after a while Anuksha's father came back over to her room. He stood near the door.

"Have you eaten your supper?" He asked.

"Yes, I have eaten." Anuksha answered from the bed.

"Good night." Father said. He walked into his room. Before closing the door he shouted at the housemaid. "Krishna, you eat your supper and go to your room to sleep. Don't wait for me. I have no place in my stomach. My stomach is already filled."

— SEVEN —

Anuksha's father took her to a departmental store next day. They walked into the ladies garment section of the departmental store. There was a huge showroom where so many costly dresses were on display in the showcases. Father told her to choose any dresses she liked from the showcase.

Anuksha was very much overwhelmed.

Father bought her two pairs of beautiful dresses according her choice. Then he bought her shoes, chocolates, perfume, a small wristwatch and so many gifts.

Then her father took out a hundred-rupee note from the bundle and put into her hand.

Anuksha refused to take but her father forced her to take.

"Don't refuse." Anuksha's father said." Otherwise I will be upset. You will enjoy with this money whatever you like you will buy with this money." He smiled cynically.

"Okay." Anuksha said calmly.

"Anuksha" Anuksha's father said. "His voice was gentle. One gentleman will visit our home at night. You will wear the new dress at night. Your new dress will make you more beautiful."

"Okay, I will wear." Anuksha said very innocently.

"You are my lovely daughter." Anuksha's father said and smiled a pleasant smile.

Anuksha didn't understand her father's dirty mind. She had no experience of life. She thought it would be very pleasurable to wear the new dress and to draw the attention of the guest.

For the moment Anuksha thought that her father is very loving and kind towards her. He is not like before. He had changed himself.

Who will visit our home at night?" Anuksha asked the housemaid.

The housemaid laughed, "Your father's new friend. His name is Pratim Dutt.

"Oh my father's new friend!" Anuksha shook her hand. "Is he polite?" She asked.

Suddenly the housemaid made such a gesture as if the question didn't please her.

"I don't know whether he is polite or not." The housemaid said. "But I can say that he is also a drunkard like your father."

With sudden Anuksha's view towards her father had changed. She almost got angry. She got the smell of any new conspiracy of her father.

At night Pratim Dutt came to their home along with her father. Her father was holding a big bottle of whisky wrapped with a silver paper.

Anuksha's father looked at Anuksha. He smiled. "She is my daughter." He introduced Anuksha to Pratim Dutt.

Pratim Dutt slowly turned towards Anuksha and threw a soft look at her. "Your daughter is so beautiful." He said pleasantly.

Anuksha was standing in a corner of the room silently. Pratim Dutt was a big built man. He wore a costly suit and his wristwatch shone.

Pratim Dutt sat down into the sofa.

"Why are you standing there, Anuksha?" Pratim Dutt said. "Please come near me."

Anuksha walked over to Pratim Dutt.

"Please sit beside me." Pratim Dutt said looking up at Anuksha.

Anuksha sat down into the sofa beside him in shy and hesitation.

Pratim Dutt took a chocolate out of his pocket and handed over to her hand.

"It is for you." Pratim Dutt said pressing Anuksha's hand.

"Thank you." Anuksha said and ran into her room.

Pratim Dutt glanced across Anuksha. He laughed, "Silly girl." He mumbled.

Anuksha removed the wrapper of the chocolate and started to eat. She thought the gentleman is very nice. Though he was father's friend but he was not like his father. He may be a clean man. She thought that the housemaid might have wrong impression about him.

A kind of curiosity grew within her to know about Pratim Dutt.

After the dinner Anuksha's father and Pratim Dutt entered into the room and locked from inside.

— EIGHT —

It was a sunny morning. Anuksha's father took Anuksha's to the market for monthly shopping. He bought her new dresses and cosmetics again. She wore one after another dress in front of the mirror and looked into her image in the mirror until she was pleased.

"Are you happy with this?" Anuksha's father asked her with a smile on his wrinkled face.

"Yes father." Anuksha answered. "I am happy."

Then Anuksha's father took her to beauty parlour to change her hair style.

"Give a new style to her hair." Anuksha's father told the beautician. "My daughter should look more beautiful"

The beautician started her work as Anuksha sat down confidently leaning her back on the chair in front of the big mirror.

At last the beautician gave a perfect and new style into Anuksha's hair.

"Now you have grown to a more beautiful girl." The beautician said smiling.

Anuksha was delighted but she disliked because her new style made her into a young lady more than a young girl.

Next day Anuksha's father got her admission in computer institute.

Sudden change in father's behaviour almost puzzled Anuksha's inexperienced mind. She didn't understand. She thought that the new dresses her father bought her would delight him when she would wear. She thought she misunderstood her father.

Often Anuksha's father brought expensive goods for her, which he never brought before for her.

Anuksha often wondered looking at her father's changing attitude towards her. But it delighted her. It is a good sign of her father.

Though Anuksha had little experience of life but slowly she discovered that he hadn't changed himself. He was the same person he was many years ago. His behavior towards her was only acting. He brought her into his trap of his dirty plan of mind.

Anuksha came to know that the new dresses, expensive goods, chocolate her father gave her were actually bought by Pratim Dutt's money. Mr. Pratim Dutt had already bought her father by his money and made him a slave. Also Anuksha came to know that her father had taken a huge amount of money from Mr. Pratim Dutt, which her father can't return in his life time. Now he had been almost like a slave of Pratim Dutta.

One night Pratim Dutt came to their home along with her father. Her father was holding a whisky bottle wrapped with a silver paper.

They entered into the room and locked from the inside.

Anuksha had a curiosity what they are doing inside the room so she came out of her room and walked over to her father's room. She silently stood near the door and peeped to the inside through the small hole of the door. She had seen the private world of her father and Pratim Dutt. She was almost strange. There was no any aroma of gentleness in their manners there was only aroma of discourtesy in their manners. The inside of the room was filled with smokes and smells of whisky.

They were drinking whisky one after another glass and gave deep puffs into their cigerattes.

Anuksha noticed that every now and then they exchanged some dirty words between each other very shamelessly and laughed.

Anuksha was shocked. Her mind was filled with hatred and anger towards her father and Pratim Dutt. She started to hate them.

"I thought that Pratim Dutt is a gentle man." Anuksha muttered to herself. "But my conception was wrong. He is also like my father."

— NINE —

Anuksha returned to her room. She switched off the light and fell asleep on the bed as soon as she lay on the bed with a bitter feeling in mind about her father and Pratim Dutt.

Same thing started to happen every night. Pratim Dutt came to their home every night along with her father. They locked themselves into her father's room and drank wine one after another glass until they finished their bottles and exchanged dirty words between them immodestly.

Pratim Dutt showed himself very kind towards Anuksha. He often brought different delicious sweets and gifts for her. She didn't want to accept them but she was afraid of her father so she accepted them but she neither ate them nor used them. She put them into a plastic bag and threw to the dustbin.

Several months later one morning Anuksha's father had been ill. Doctors told that due to drinking of alcohol his liver had been damaged. He was hospitalized. He spent many weeks in the hospital bed until he was well.

Since then Anuksha's father was often ill. So she gave up her study and began to nurse her father.

Anuksha didn't like her father. She didn't like the life she was leading. She was weary and worn out. She wanted to escape from home but where to escape she didn't know. The housemaid was very loving towards her. She always encouraged her.

Anuksha looked at her father. His face was wrinkled. His beards started greying. He had been old before time. Alcohol had finished his life. What was his age? He was only fourty two. Most of his friends were still young.Then suddenly a fear shook her little heart what will happen to her if he died? What she will do? She had sudden feeling of insecurity thinking an uncertain future.

There was knock on the door. Anuksha went over to the door and opened it. Mr. Pratim Dutt was there. He came in. He wore a black suit and black tie. He was holding a small packet in his hand. He smiled.

"How are you, Anuksha?" Pratim Dutt asked.

"Fine," Anuksha answered unwillingly.

"How is your father now?" Mr. Pratim Dutt asked.

"Little better," Anuksha answered.

"Let's go to your room." Pratim Dutt said.

Mr. Pratim Dutt followed Anuksha to her room. He sat down on the edge of the bed. He glanced up at her.

"Take it." Pratim Dutt said holding out the small packet to her, "A small gift for you."

Pratim Dutt held Anuksha's hand as she took the small packet from him.He gazed at her. His gaze was lustful.

"Please let me go now." Anuksha said. "I am too tired now."

But Pratim Dutt didn't allow her to go. He swiftly put his arm around her and pulled her to him. He kissed her almost passionately.

Anuksha was very much ashamed and afraid. She didn't like him. She hated him since the night she saw him to drink alcohol with her father and exchanging dirty words between them.

Pratim Dutt held her more tightly than before and he tried to kiss her lips as she struggled to free herself from him.

"Don't be silly, Anuksha." Pratim Dutt said. "I love you. I am ready to sacrifice my life for you. Really I love you. Please don't refuse me. Let me kiss you again and again. You have made me crazy."

Anuksha was scared if the housemaid came and saw them.

"Please let me go." Anuksha said almost angrily.

"Okay." Pratim said. He freed her, as he was pleased to kiss her.

Pratim Dutt walked out of the room lighting a cigarette. Anuksha closed the door. She stood in front of the mirror and looked her face. Her face was almost red denned.

The housemaid came to Anuksha's room after a while. She asked her if anything happened to her.

"Nothing," Anuksha answered calmly. "Has Pratim Dutt gone?" She asked.

"Yes he has gone just now." The housemaid answered. He looked very pleased.

Anuksha went to the bathroom. She rubbed her face properly with palm and washed her face with cold water from the tap.

Anuksha couldn't sleep that night. Her mind was troubled. She got up very early in the morning and went out to the street.

So many morning walkers were walking in the street. Some of them were holding sticks in hands to drive away the stray dogs.

Anuksha walked down the street for an hour. Then she realized that she had come long way and it was time to go back home.

Slowly one by one many vehicles started to appear in the street. Long distant passengers were running to catch the morning train towards their destinations. Sweepers started to sweep the street with their long brooms.

Anuksha was tired and hungry. She returned home. The housemaid already got up and started her morning works. She was cleaning the utensils in the kitchen's basin.

"Where did you go Anuksha in this early morning?" The housemaid asked.

"For morning walk." Anuksha answered.

"Now you brush your teeth and wash your face." The housemaid said. I will complete breakfast for you and your father within half an hour."

"Don't awake father now." Anuksha said. "Let him sleep until it is eight O'clock. He needs more sleep.

Six months later. It was about 9 O'clock at night. It was raining. With sudden Anuksha's father had been ill again.

Anuksha was almost afraid. She was nervous. She couldn't make up her mind what to do. Then she went out opening an umbrella over her head to bring a doctor leaving the house maid beside her father to look after him.

A few moments later Anuksha came back along with a local doctor.

The doctor prescribed some medicines and left after initial check up and told her to take much care of her father.

For several days Anuksha hardly left her father's bedside. The doctor told that her father's condition was not good. She was afraid. Only one fear disturbed her mind what will happen to her if her father dies. In time no one to stand beside her. She remembered Anupam where he may be now. He didn't leave any address for her even to write a letter to him to tell her pathetic story.

— TEN —

Anuksha tried to avoid Pratim Dutt. But he gave much importance on her than her ill father. His look was lustful.

Pratim Dutt threw a long glance at Anuksha. Craftiness smiled on his face.

"Why don't you speak to me, Anuksha?" Pratim Dutt asked. "Why are you avoiding me?"

Anuksha was silent.

Pratim Dutt softly grasped Anuksha's hand. "Are you angry?" He asked. "Don't be silly."

Anuksha didn't say anything.

"Anuksha," Pratim Dutt said. His tone was almost soft. "I want to ask you something, Anuksha. I don't know whether you will like it or not. But I hope to get a positive answer from you."

After long silence Anuksha opened her mouth "Ask quickly what you want to ask me?" Anuksha said in anger. "I have no time. I am in hurry. It is time to give medicine to my father."

"Will you marry me?" Pratim Dutt asked suddenly. His face was brightened with excitement.

Anuksha was never ready to hear such a proposal from him. But she knew that he would ask her such a question, which was not acceptable for her.

Anuksha quickly refused his proposal.

Pratim Dutt was still grasping her hand. And Anuksha wanted to free her hand from his grasp and escape from there.

Then Pratim Dutt slowly loosened his grasp from Anuksha's hand. He laughed almost like a hypocrite looking at her face.

"You are still angry with me." Pratim Dutt said. "I am ready to accept any punishment you give me. But don't hurt my tiny heart." He gazed at her face in such a way as if his eyes will devour her face.

"I always wanted to tell you about this." Pratim Dutt said. "Your father also knows it very well. If you marry me then you will be happy forever. I will give you anything you want to eat anything you want to wear. You will rule like a queen."

"I wouldn't marry you." Anuksha mumbled to herself. "You are the most hatred person for me."

Anuksha didn't dare to say it to her father. After Pratim Dutt left their home she told the matter to the housemaid.

"How Pratim Dutt dared to tell me to marry him?" Anuksha said. "I will tell it to my father."

The housemaid laughed, "You silly girl." She said. "I knew it that one day Pratim Dutt will give you such a proposal to marry him. What is the use of telling it to your father? Your father already had been slave of him. Your father has no power to tell against him. He had bought your father. Your father had borrowed a huge amount of money from him which he can't return in his life time."

Anuksha was shocked. She almost broke down. "I don't like my father." She said weeping. "I hate my father."

The housemaid lulled Anuksha. "Don't weep Anuksha. Keep patience. This is your bad luck that you have got such a father who can throw his own daughter to the hell for his own benefit."

"Now you eat your meal." The housemaid said. "Forget all these. Don't take much tension. It will affect your health."

A few days later Anuksha's father's health gradually improved. He had been much better than before.

The housemaid served dinner both Anuksha and her father at the dining table together.

For the first time both Anuksha and her father sat at the dining table and ate together. She hardly remembered her father sat to eat with her together.

During their eating Anuksha's father put his hand on Anuksha's shoulder. He slowly turned his eyes at her.

"Anuksha" her father's tone was soft and kind, "Will you marry Mr. Pratim Dutt?" He asked. "I think already he had given the proposal to you."

Anuksha didn't say anything. Her bloods were boiling in anger.

"Pratim Dutt is a rich man." Anuksha's father said. "You will be happy if you marry him. He can give you all the luxuries you want."

Anuksha was burning in anger. She wanted to pour her all hatred on her father. She couldn't finish her meal. She left the dining table and went to her room. She shut the door from inside and lay on the bed pressing her face on the pillow.

Anuksha began to think that how a father can force his daughter to marry a man who is her father's age, whom she hates most. Tears slowly filled her eyes. Then she could realize that what the housemaid told was true. Her father knew everything about that.

Anuksha jumped out of the bed. She sat at the table and took a white copy out of the shelf and started to write to Anupam without knowing his address and where to send the letter. She finished one after another page until she finished all the pages of the white copy almost like a mad woman. She remembered Anupam every now and then. She wanted to cry out—Anupam where are you? You come and rescue me from the torment of this life."

Next morning Anuksha's father came to Anuksha's room. He looked around before looking at Anuksha.

"I have given you some days to think about the matter. Anuksha's father said. "I hope you will not deny. By the way Mr. Pratim Dutt sent a beautiful dress for you. You will wear the dress when he will come to our home. He will be happy to see you in the new dress."

— ELEVEN —

Anuksha felt broken. Nothing could comfort her. She wanted to kill herself. She only wept and wept and remembered Anupam. The man whom she loved, the man whom she always wanted to marry had gone to a foreign country. Even she didn't know his whereabouts to write a letter to express her misery.

Pratim Dutt came that night. He wore a nice coat. He was clean shaved and he used colour on his shortly cut hair. He tried to make himself younger than his age.

Anuksha's father ordered the housemaid to cook mutton for the dinner, which was Mr. Pratim Dutt's favourite dish.

Mr. Pratim Dutt brought lots of gifts wrapped with colourful papers for Anuksha. He kept the gifts on the table in Anuksha's room. But she didn't touch them.

Anuksha's father told Anuksha to wear the new dress brought by Mr. Pratim Dutt for her.

"Anuksha," Anuksha's father said smiling. "You will look very beautiful in your new dress. I think you will like my choice. Don't refuse my request"

Anuksha felt her bloods were boiling. But she couldn't turn down her father's order. She said yes lightly shaking her head. She put on the new dress given to her by Pratim Dutt.

Anuksha's father and Pratim Dutt had already finished one bottle of whisky among the three bottles they brought for the night. They were almost drunk.

The housemaid set dinner on the dining table. Anuksha's father and Pratim Dutt sat at the dining table. Anuksha's father told the housemaid to call Anuksha to the dining table to eat dinner together with them.

The housemaid went into Anuksha's room and called her to the dining table to eat dinner with them.

When Anuksha walked over to the dining table and sat opposite them. Mr. Pratim Dutt gazed at her. "You are looking so beautiful." He said with a very pleasant smile.

Mr. Pratim Dutt gazed again at her face. He didn't take away his gaze from her face for a long time.

"Your daughter is really very beautiful." Pratim Dutt said to Anuksha's father.

Anuksha's father laughed a proud laugh. "Remember she is my daughter. She is Mr. Arindom's daughter." He said proudly beating his bony chest.

"Do you know what makes your daughter's beauty more perfect than other girls?" Pratim Dutt asked suddenly.

"No!" Anuksha's father answered. There was enough wonder in his eyes.

"Your daughter's beauty has softness and sweetness." Pratim Dutt said.

They both burst into laughter almost very shamelessly.

"Truly your daughter is so pretty and charming. Her beauty has a heavenly touch." Pratim Dutt said.

Anuksha didn't say anything. She was standing silently like a lifeless body with anger and pain before them. She felt herself as if a piece of flesh thrown before a hungry dog.

"Anuksha," Anuksha's father said slowly turning his look at her. "You have to marry Mr. Pratim Dutt. I hope you won't refuse. Pratim Dutt is a very nice man. He has a kind heart. I am so grateful to him. He had great contribution in my life."

Anuksha's throat went dry and stiff. She had no courage to refuse her father but she had to agree with him. With sudden her tiny heart was shuddered as she remembered once her father beat her mercilessly when she refused his order in her childhood.

There was a long silence.

"Look at me, Anuksha." Anuksha's father said.

As she slowly raised her eyes up and looked at him she was almost frightened. His eyes were burning in anger and for the first time she had seen such anger in his eyes.

"Don't refuse me." Anuksha's father almost threatened her.

Pratim Dutt threw a soft glance at her. "Anuksha" He said. Now you go to your room. I hope you will think the matter very sincerely what your father has told you. I hope you will not hurt your father.

Anuksha suddenly felt her all blood frozen. She ran into her room. She broke down to tears. She thought for the moment that better she should die than marrying Pratim Dutt. It was just like a nightmare for her.

Anuksha tried to forget the nightmare. She tried to lighten her burdened mind. So she remembered Anupam. Then her memories with Anupam were the only source of inspirations to lighten the burden of her mind. She remembered once both of them were traveling in a bus. Anupam was sitting beside her. She fell into asleep leaning her head on his shoulder and he put an arm around her and held comfortably. That was a wonderful journey for her to remember forever. They wore same colour dresses. The jolly conductor of the bus threw a glance at them and passed a comment "Made for each other." He smiled and went away. Then every passenger inside the bus burst out laughing looking at them and they were blushed.

Anuksha's heart cried out for Anupam. Her weary heart wanted him madly. There was no one of her own to explain what was going inside her heart.

Anuksha heard loud voices of her father and Pratim Dutt. They were talking and laughing loudly. They were smoking and enjoying drinks themselves. Every now and then they made some jokes and burst out laughing.

Anuksha switched off the light and lay in darkness on the bed.

"Father, I won't marry Pratim Dutt." Anuksha mumbled to herself. "I hate him. I don't want to see his face. Father, why are you sending your daughter to live in hell?"

In the morning Anuksha put on her dress and went out to the milk booth to bring milk, which she always brought for her ill father. Though her father didn't like milk yet she forced him to drink for his health.

There was long queue in front of the milk booth. Anuksha stood in the queue. Then her look went across the street and with sudden to her surprise her eyes saw Anupam walking down the street. Her heart filled with joy and excitement. She hurriedly walked out of the queue and started to run after Anupam.

Her eyes shone with profound joy. How much she was glad to see him it was beyond imagination.

For her it was a miracle of god. She never thought that she will meet her love again. She thought she will die bit by bit in mental anguish. It was a reconciliation of two souls and two hearts. It was a reunification of her love. She thanked god for being benevolent and kind on her.

"Anupam, Anupam." Anuksha shouted and ran after him as if she had found her lost stars.

Anupam heard her voice. He stopped. He slowly turned around and looked back at Anuksha. As he saw Anuksha his eyes shone with excitement "Anuksha." He almost cried out.

Tears came out of Anuksha's eyes as her eyes met Anupam's eyes after long years. It was a very emotional and joyful moment for them. She closed her eyes and thanked to god again for reconciliation.

There was a long silence between them. They lost their words in excitement and joy and emotions caught their breaths.

"Anuksha," Anupam said.

Anuksha couldn't say anything. She had a feeling that her body has been frozen. She was weeping silently.

"Don't weep, Anuksha." Anupam lulled her. "I am so sorry. I suddenly went to Kuwait without giving you address."

Anuksha was silent. She thought he was the first man in her life whom she loved with heart and soul whom she wanted to get forever. But he suddenly disappeared from her life but now he had appeared when everything is finished in her life to offer him.

Anuksha looked at his face with a sort of fascination. "Anupam," She whispered. "You can't feel my joy, Joy of meeting you. Joy of meeting the man I love most. My thirsty heart and soul are quenched after long years." Tears rushed to her eyes again.

Anupam slowly put his arm around her. He softly kissed on her head. And his soft kiss how comforted her she had no word to explain.

They went to a park nearby. They sat down on a long wooden table in a corner of the park. The morning sunlight shone the whole park as if new hope coming to their lives.

Anuksha laid her head on his shoulder. She told him everything about her life living there and he was pained to hear all.

Anupam took her face between hands and stared into her eyes.

"Why don't you defy father?" Anupam asked.

Anuksha had no word to answer. He was almost dumb.

"Why?" Anupam asked.

"I don't dare to defy father." Anuksha answered. "I am afraid of my father."

"You know, Anuksha." Anupam said holding her face close. "No one has right to force you to marry a man whom you don't like. It is a crime."

"What can I do now?" Anuksha asked like a kid." It is too late.I have already given word to my father."

"You know, Pratim Dutt is your father's age." Anupam said. "You will never be happy with him."

"I know that." Anuksha shook her head.

After a silence of a moment Anupam stared at her.

"Why are you going to ruin your life?" Anupam asked.

"Now there is no meaning of living for me." Anuksha said. "Let me ruin my life."

"Don't say like that." Anupam said.

"I haven't seen any light in the path of my life." Anuksha said. "I have seen only dark coming ahead."

"There is light in the path of your life." Anupam said. "But you have to find that."

"Forgive me, Anupam." Anuksha said apologetically looking at him. "Now I am feeling that someone is piercing a knife through my heart. It is called destiny. She took a long sigh. No one can change one's destiny. It was written with birth. By the way when had you returned to Calcutta from Kuwait?" She asked.

"Four months ago." Anupam answered. I went there in four years contract to work for an oil company.

"What are you doing now?" Anuksha asked.

"Now I am working for a 'NGO'." Anupam answered.

"You know, Anupam." Anuksha said. Her tone had emotions. "After you left for Kuwait I went to your maternal uncle's home to know about you."

"Did you remember me in those years?" Anupam asked.

"Every moment I remembered you." Anuksha answered. Do you believe how I wanted you in those years? How much tears I had wasted for you? My heart always cried for you."

"Thank God." Anupam said. "God is benevolent. God has given the opportunity to meet you again. Believe me I always remembered you."

"Believe me." Anuksha said. "I always remembered you too. I always wanted to write letter to you. But you didn't leave any address to contact you. How can I forget you when your love is flowing in my veins?"

"I am really feeling guilty for that." Anupam said. "After returning from Kuwait I went to Neena aunt's home in Darjeeling to enquire about you. There I have come to know that your father had taken you back to Jadavpur after class twelve results. I was very much hurt"

"Now we will meet regularly." Anuksha said. A smile of joy and happiness appeared in her lips after a long time. "You have brought my lost smile back to my lips after long time." She said.

"Now I am staying at my home". Anupam said. "And my office is at Jadavpur." He smiled.

They hugged each other and walked out of the park to the street after sharing some affectionate moments.

— TWELVE —

Anuksha went back to the milk booth. But by that time the milk booth was already closed. On her way to home she walked into a shop by the street to buy a piece of detergent soap. She got a scrubber free with the piece of detergent soap and she was happy.

Anuksha told lie to her father that the milk booth was closed for that day so she couldn't bring milk and her father believed it.

Anuksha's mind was full of joy after meeting Anupam. She was humming songs every now and then. She thought now she could meet him regularly and that thought brought a thrill to her mind.

Next afternoon Anuksha went out of home and met Anupam near the park where he was waiting for an hour for her.

They walked into the park together and sat on a bench. They spent there for a while then they came out of the park and boarded a bus towards Chowringhee. They sat near the window slightly leaning their heads on the seat looking out. They were silent. So many thoughts came to his mind and wanted to speak something to her. But He was also silent as if. He lost his mind somewhere in a deep sea of dream.

Anuksha thought god has opened his eyes on her at last. Today god has given her an opportunity to board a bus together with him.

"Where are we going now?" Anuksha asked him suddenly.

"We are going to Chowringhee." Anupam answered. "Very soon we will reach our destination. Don't worry."

A few minutes later the bus conductor started to shout Chowringhee, Chowringhee as the bus arrived Chowringhee. They quickly got off the bus.

They started walking on the footpath holding each other's hands.

"So many things I have to tell you Anupam." Anuksha said laying her head over his shoulder.

"Tell." Anupam said softly.

"I was very much anxious when I will see you again."
Anuksha said. "I had spent so many sleepless nights
for you. How much I cried for you. You can't imagine
that."

"I was also very much anxious to see you again."
Anupam said. "It is true that I went to Kuwait but
I left my heart and soul in you." He put his arm
around her. He kissed her on the head.

"You can't imagine how I spent those four years."
Anuksha said. "I wanted you madly every moment. I
was restless to hear a word from you."

"I can feel your pain, Anuksha." Anupam said. "Now
forget the past like a nightmare." You can't bring
back the past."

I know I can't bring back the past." Anuksha said.
"I try to forget the past like a nightmare but I can't.
They come back again like pet animals."

"You can, Anuksha you can." Anupam said tightening
his arm around her. "Now look at the evening sun.
What a wonderful! How the evening sun is spreading
red beams on the earth with a new promise to come
back again in the tomorrow morning."

"Anuksha looked up at the round and red sun.
"Wonderful!" She said. "Today we have wonderful
evening because we are together." She smiled gladly.

"Yes Of course." Anupam said.

They walked and talked a lot each other. They talked many topics. Anupam told about a funny incident happened with him in Kuwait. She burst into laughter.

Time had come to go back. Time didn't permit them to spend more time. They boarded a bus.

Anuksha's heart cried out as she said him good-bye.

Anuksha stood on the street for a long time looking across Anupam until he disappeared into the crowd. She felt very cold and slowly started to walk back towards home.

Anuksha's father was at home. He stared at her as she entered to the house.

"Where did you go?" Anuksha's father asked.

"I went to one of my friend's home." Anuksha answered almost timidly.

"But I don't like you to go to any friend's home." Anuksha's father said. "And I don't want you to stay in the outside till the evening."

Anuksha's father never allowed Anuksha to talk with any boy. He feared if she eloped with someone. So he always threatened her not to meet any boy.

Then Anuksha's father changed himself. He looked at Anuksha very calmly.

"I want to talk to you." Anuksha's father said. His voice was soft. "Come near me and sit beside me."

Anuksha walked over to him and stood beside him politely.

"Sit beside me." Anuksha's father said.

"No thanks." Anuksha said.

"Remember, now you are not a girl." Anuksha's father said. "You are going to be a young woman now. Every girl becomes a woman after marriage and you are going to marry Pratim Dutt very soon. So don't spend much time outside home talking with others."

Anuksha's throat went dry. She felt that she had lost the ground under her feet.

"It is your good time." Anuksha's father said. "You are going to marry a nice and rich man. Your life will shine like a star."

"Father you are wrong." Anuksha said to herself. "My life is not going to shine like a star. My life is going to ruin like a poor girl who has no aspiration; no dream no hope to live her way. She has to live like a caged bird until her death.

Anuksha's father stared at Anuksha.

"Pratim Dutt is a gentleman." He said. "His heart is very kind. I am sure you will be happy with him." He smiled.

Anuksha slowly shut her eyes. "Father," She said to herself. "I am very unfortunate. I lost my mother one and half years after my birth. Though I have a father but who never gave fatherly love and took care of his daughter."

"Come on, Anuksha, come on." Anuksha's father said. "His voice was irritable. "Why don't you speak anything? Don't be silly, my child. You should be happy that you are going to marry a nice and rich man, where you can rule like a queen."

"What to say?" Anuksha asked.

"How are you feeling about your marriage?" Father asked.

"Nothing," Anuksha answered softly.

"Aren't you happy?" Anuksha's father asked almost angrily.

Anuksha was silent. She wanted to cry.

"Don't be silly." Anuksha's father said. "He will love you very much."

"I have no one to love me in this world." Anuksha said almost sadly.

With sudden Anuksha's father changed himself to an emotional father. He put his hand on Anuksha's shoulder.

"Anuksha don't say like this." Anuksha's father said. "Don't hurt your father. I am your father and I love you. Pratim Dutt is a very lovable person. He loves you too much. You will be very happy with him. You will see how he will give love to you after marriage even you will forget your father. He smiled. But don't forget your father. Your father has no one look after him. Only you are my last hope so you do as I say."

"Are you happy now my good daughter?" He patted on her shoulder.

Anuksha nodded her head unwillingly.

— THIRTEEN —

As the Anuksha's wedding day was coming near, her heart beats started to pound heavily. Her mind was upset as if she was going to end her life.

She never saw her father to be happy before. He was full of joy in heart. He was always around her. Every now and then he sang songs in joy and did little fun with her.

"You are my lovely daughter." Anuksha's father said. You will look like princess on the wedding day. By the way you don't go out until your marriage is completed. It is inauspicious.

Anuksha never gave her father to know how much she was unhappy to marry Pratim Dutt. She sacrificed her all dreams and wishes of life for him.

She didn't want to hurt her father any more better she should hurt herself.

One month before the wedding day some relatives of Pratim Dutt came to Anuksha's home. They brought golden ornaments, costly sarees, sweets, fishes, and lots of sweets for the bride. Among the golden ornaments were two pairs of necklace set with precious diamonds, one diamond ring, three pairs of ear rings, ten pairs of golden bungles and other so many things.

One of Pratim Dutt's relatives told Anuksha that Pratim Dutt is a very rich man. He has lots of plans after marriage. He will buy a new flat and car for her and he will take her to Goa for honeymoon after marriage.

Nothing could give real pleasure to her sad heart. Nothing could fix the crack in her heart. Sometimes she wept hiding her face with two hands. Once she dreamt of a lively future but now that was dead.

As the wedding day came near she noticed a vast change in her father's behaviour. He was no more an angry man rather he was polite, kind and cordial. He behaved with her like a devoted father.

Then one week before the wedding day suddenly Pratim Dutt came to their home. He was drunk. Even he could not stand properly. Anuksha's father was not at home that time. Anuksha was almost frightened. She locked herself in her room. Pratim Dutt shouted at her to open the door but she didn't open the door. "Anuksa," He said. Please open the door. You are going to be my wife. I want to kiss you. Please don't hurt my heart."

"Please now you go." Anuksha said. "Now you are drunk and I don't like a drunkard."

Then Anuksha exchanged some hot arguments with Pratim Dutt before he left their home.

Anuksha never expected such behaviour from the man who would be her husband one week later. She cried all the nights. She could see dark clouds coming ahead to her life.

Next morning Pratim Dutt came to Anuksha's home with so many gifts for her. He apologized for what happened last night.

The house was painted with new colour. New flower vases took place in the place of old one in the table. The windows and doors got new curtains. The whole house got a new look. Her father did everything himself, which he never did before.

The relatives around the city and outside the city crowded the home. There was a merry environment in the home.

The wedding day had come. Anuksha was fasting from the morning. She was bathed with turmeric paste. After that she wore a costly saree. She wore golden bungles along with conch bangles into her two hands for long life of her husband. Then she wore golden necklace, diamond rings and golden earrings and so on. Her whole body was adorned with golden ornaments. She looked like a golden bride. A hired beautician gave a beautiful style to her hair and heavy makeup shone her face brightly and vermilion adorned her forehead. A vast change came to her whole personality. She was no more a girl. She had been a young and beautiful woman.

Anuksha was taken to the wedding place in the evening.

At about eight O'clock bridegroom Pratim Dutt had arrived the wedding hall along with a long convoy of cars.

Music started and the guests began to dance in the wedding hall

Next day in the evening it was time for Anuksha to leave her father's home to her husband Pratim Dutt's home. She looked very sad. Her eyes were filled with tears and the mind was full of melancholy.

"Anuksha," Anuksha's father said. His tone was very calm. "Forgive me if I have done any wrong to you." Suddenly tears shone his eyes.

For the first time Anuksha saw tears in her father's eyes. Though she hated her father yet she had pain for her father for that moment to leave her father alone.

Anuksha looked twice back at the home where she grew up before entering into the car. Then she looked at her father and the housemaid. She couldn't stop her tears. Tears rolled down her cheeks profusely.

On the way to Pratim Dutt's home the car stopped near a temple. Both Anuksha and Putul Dutt got off the car. They stood with folding hands before the greater image of goddess Kali and took blessings for a happy married life.

"Are you happy with this marriage?" Pratim Dutt asked.

Anuksha was silent looking out very indifferently. Tears brightened her eyes silently.

Pratim Dutt drew her close and he tried to console her. "It happens to every girl." He said, "Each and every girl has to leave father's home one day and goes to husband's home. It is the truth and it is the custom of our society."

— FOURTEEN —

Anuksha and Pratim Dutt went to Goa for their honeymoon. "Goa beaches are wonderful for the honeymoon couple and I had a long plan to come here after marriage" Pratim Dutt said.

Honeymoon was a bitter experience for Anuksha. What she thought about honeymoon that never happened. From the honeymoon night she started to feel that another phase of suffering is going to begin in her life which will end with the end of her life.

Anuksha spent the eveing alone in the hotel room. She didn't know where Pratim Dutt was and what was he doing.

Then to her surprise after ten O'clock at night Pratim Dutt returned to the hotel room along with a woman near about fourty. He was drunk. He introduced the woman with Anuksha.

"She is my friend of many years." Pratim Dutt said. "After she got married we always exchanged letters between each other. I have met her after a long time. She is also coming to Goa to spend her holiday. Don't mind." He laughed. Today I will spend the night with her. And he left the hotel room putting a hand around the woman's neck. "Good night Anuksha."

Every night Anuksha was alone in the hotel room and Pratim Dutt spent the nights with the woman. Every night she wanted to kill herself but how? The next moment she changed her mind.

Anuksha couldn't endure it anymore and she had a quarrel with Pratim Dutt violently.

"You are a man of dirty character." Anuksha shouted angrily. If you have to spend the nights with other woman then why did you marry me?" She asked. "You are not fit to be a husband."

But Pratim Dutt had no reaction. Only he laughed.

"You have no right to interfere in my personal life." Pratim Dutt said. "I have married you so it is not that I am your slave. Women have no right to say anything on their husband whatever they do."

Pratim Dutt started to abuse her with dirty words which she never heard in her life. There was no any alternative way for her except crying.

"You bitch." Suddenly he said. He gave a slap on her face and went out of the room.

Anuksha lay on the bed. She pressed her face into the pillow and started crying. She blamed her father, she blamed her destiny.

Anuksha dreamt of a beautiful honeymoon. But now she realized that was not written on her destiny. Some dirty words and a slap on the face were written on her destiny as a honeymoon gifts from husband.

They spent about fifteen days in Goa. Every day they did quarrel each other. Anuksha went out to the sea beach alone and spent long hours there walking by the sea. The pristine beaches overwhelmed her.

After returning from the honeymoon they shifted to a new flat he bought two weeks after the marriage at Chowringhee. New furniture, new curtains adorned the new flat.

Anuksha was still very young and ignorant. She had no long experience of life. Pratim Dut was an experienced man, who had experience of fifty years of life. So there was a vast difference in their mentality.

Already one year had gone. That one year was very awful for her. In that one year she never enjoyed joy and happiness of married life. Anuksha marriage to Pratim Dut was a tragedy. Then another tragedy was waiting for her. One night suddenly Pratim Dutt had a severe heart attack. He was rushed to the hospital in an ambulance but he had died before he reached the hospital.

Another blow, another nightmare was waiting to hit her broken life. Only six months passed after her husband died then one day again Anuksha was forced by her father to marry Pratim Dutt's younger brother Putul Dutt who was working as a manager in a private company in Bombay. She thought he will not be like his elder brother. He will understand his wife's feelings. But she was wrong. Her luck was bad. He was also a drunkard and abusive like his elder brother.

There was not a single day Putul Dutt didn't abuse her. Every now and then Putul Dutt abused her as if he found kind of pleasure to abuse her. Abuse had been like a part of her everyday life.

"You bitch." Putul Dutt shouted at her. "You have killed my elder brother. You are responsible for my elder brother's death. I know now you will kill me. You are an inauspicious woman."

Anuksha had no word to answer. She only cried. She blamed her luck. She thought that she was born very unlucky as if she was born to suffer only the bitterness of life.

— FIFTEEN —

When Anuksha cried then Putul Dutt tried to console her. He apologized to her for his fault and he promised not to hurt her again but he forgot everything the next moment.

The life was becoming worse as the days went on. Sometimes he suddenly disappeared for two or three days from home without saying her anything. When he was asked then he told lie. He told her that he went out of the city for business purpose.

Putul Dutt was still leading the life he led before marriage. There had been no any change in his life style.

Putul Dutt was always irritated by every word Anuksha said. He always tried to find fault what she said or did.

Occasionally Putul Dutt took out Anuksha for dinner in the hotels. He took her for shopping and he bought her beautiful gifts

One evening Putul Dutt brought a bottle of whisky. He took a glass from the shelf and sat at the dining table. He opened the cork and poured whisky into the glass and drank down at once. Then he started to drink one after another glass then Anuksha came and stood before him and looked at him angrily and told him to stop drinking.

But next moment Putul Dutt jumped out of the chair. He swiftly caught her hair and started beating her mercilessly. She fell down on the floor with a little injury on the face. She cried profusely.

"You promised me to be kind and loving." Anuksha said. "You told me that you will love me forever but now you have beaten me." She wailed.

"I am sorry, Anuksha." Putul Dutt said. He apologized. He put his hand around her and hugged affectionately. He kissed her "Anuksha I can't tolerate any one who interfere my freedom." He said in a soft tone almost like a psychic patient.

"I am not interfereing your freedom." Anuksha said. "I have just told you to give up this bad habit. Do you think this is good for your health?" She asked.

Putul Dutt laughed. "I know that." He said. "You know Anuksha I am addicted to drinking wine. I can't live without it whether you like it or not. But I can't give up it." He laughed again.

Anuksha didn't say anything. She gave a look at his eyes silently.

"All right," Putul Dutt said nodding his head, "I will try."

One evening sudden illness weakened Anuksha. She lay on the bed and started groaning in stomachache. But Putul Dutt didn't look at her. He didn't show any sympathy to her. He hurriedly went out of home. Before going out he told her to be careful about herself. He told that he will consult a doctor and he will bring medicine for her and also he promised to come back soon.

But Putul Dutt broke his promise. Anuksha was waiting when he would come and bring medicine for her. It had been nine O'clock at night. Still there was no any trace of him.

It was about ten O'clock when Putul Dutt entered home mumbling something indistinctly. He was drunk and he was holding a bottle of wine in his hand instead of medicine for her.

"You are still lying on the bed." Putul Dutt said.

Anuksha didn't give any answer. She was lying giving her back to Pratim Dutt.

Putul Dutt came near her and sat on the bed beside her still holding the bottle of wine in hand. "Are you angry with me?" He asked.

Anuksha was silent. Smell of alcohol struck her nostrils. She was almost to vomit; she slowly turned her face at him. She glanced up at him furiously. "Where is my medicine?" She asked.

"I am sorry darling." Putul Dutt said. "I have forgotten. Don't mind. I will bring your medicine tomorrow morning."

"When I will die then you will bring medicine for me?" Anuksha asked.

"Don't be angry, my darling." Putul dutt said touching her forehead. "Drink little wine from my bottle then you will be cured very soon. Remember wine is the best medicine for any kind of disease." He laughed.

Anuksha didn't say anything. She felt her bloods were boiling.

Putul Dutt was continiously doing meaningless talks to her but she had no any word from her mouth. She thought what the use of talking with him is. It is better to be silent than talking with him.

"Don't you hear me Anuksha?" Putul Dutt asked her angrily. He dragged out her from the bed to the floor and started to beat her.

"Kill me." Anuksha shouted crying loudly. "I don't want to live anymore. I want to die."

"You bitch." Putul Dutt said. Suddenly he hit her with his elbow and she fell almost unconscious. He felt nervous what to do now.

Half an hour leter Anuksha slowly opened her eyes. She was still lying of the floor. Anuksha felt very weak. She couldn't raise her head. She groaned. She had a pain in the right side of her head. She thought what a husband she has got who had no any affection and care towards her.

In the next morning when Anuksha got up from the bed then she looked around. Putul Dutt was not at home. She went into the bathroom. She brushed her teeth and washed her face with cold splashes of water in her face.

Anuksha walked into the kitchen and made a cup of coffee. She still felt the pain on her head. So after drinking hot coffee she swallowed a pain killer tablet with a half glass of water. She opened the window and stood there looking at the pedestrians in the street.

There was no any trace of Putul Dutt till the noon. Still she didn't get total relief from the pain in the head. She got dressed and went to a nearby doctor. The doctor prescribed her two medicines to take twice daily.

Putul Dutt returned home in the evening. He was fully drunk. He started quarreling with her as he entered into the home. Gradually their quarrel reached such a position so that the neighbors were disturbed. Neighbors rushed to their home and threatened Putul Dutt to lodge a complaint in the police station against him. They blamed her father to allow her to marry a drunkard like him.

Anuksha was very much ashamed and hurt. She hurriedly ran into the kitchen and brought a knife and gave it to Putul Dutt's hand.

"Kill me with this knife." Anuksha shouted wailing. "I don't want to live any more with you. I am tired of this married life."

Putul Dutt was silent. He was looking at her almost vacantly.

— SIXTEEN —

It was winter, Anuksha's favorite season. The sunlights were sweet and gaiety. The mornings were cold and full of mist. She was waiting to deliver her baby. Then it was month of January when their daughter was born.

It was a wonderful moment she had never before in life. She was overwhelmed. She got the taste of motherhood and her profound joy filled her heart.

She was a lovely girl. Everyone in the neighborhood loved her. Everyone said that she was like Anuksha. But for Anuksha her daughter was more pretty and charming than her.

Her hairs were blond. Her eyes were bright, big and round. Her tiny lips were as red as red rose. Her nose was sharp and long.

When Anuksha looked down at her little daughter then her heart filled with extreme joy that was unexpressive, only she could feel that. She didn't want to go away from her even for a moment.when she looked at the innocent face of her daughter then she forgot all sufferings of life.

Putul Dutt felt himself as a proud father. Slowly his behaviour towards Anuksha started to change. He took care of both Anuksha and daughter. Sometimes sudden change in his behaviour made her strange. She knew that it was only acting.

Anuksha's father was also very happy. He often visited Anuksha's home to see his little granddaughter though he was ill. He brought dolls for her in a bag everytime he came.

Anuksha's times were filled by her daughter. She got inspiration from her daughter for living. When her daughter was asleep on the arms then she stared down at her innocent and soft face with so many wonders and dreams.

Days passed and Anuprerana grew up to a beautiful girl. Putul Dutt was very much pleased at his daughter's beauty.

"My daughter is ten times more beautiful than you." Putul Dutt said proudly to Anuksha. "I want her to walk in my path."

Putul Dutt was still in his own way. He still didn't change himself completely though Anuksha thought that he would change himself after the daughter was born.

Putul Dutt again began to come home late and drunk at night and he abused Anuksha with dirty words and he always told her to die.

Anuksha didn't say anything. She said to herself that I don't want to die now. Now I have a daughter to live. She is my inspiration. She is the part of my heart.

Anuprerana began to show good and bright sign of life as she grew up. She loved her mother very much. Anuksha was always careful about her. She feared if she inherits her father's behaviour so when her father took her for long walk then she always kept a strict watch on him, what he is talking to her what he is advising her.

Anuksha always wanted her daughter by her. She couldn't live without seeing her daughter even for a minute. She was the joy of her heart.

When Anuprerana had any ailment then Anuksha used to go mad. She ran to the doctor and consulted about the ailment. She was always beside her day and night until she fully recovered. She prayed to god for her quick recovery.It was a mother's selfless prayer to god.

By then one day when Anuprerana was about three years old then Anuksha's father had been suddenly ill.His condition was almost serious. His liver was damaged. Doctor said that there was no hope of survival for him anymore. He had a last wish before death. He wanted to see his granddaughter before death.

Anuksha took daughter Anuprerana to the hospital where her father was admitted. He held Anuprerana's tiny hand with a kind grip and looked at her affectionately. Then he looked up at Anuksha. His eyes were filled with tears.

"Anuksha," Father said very weakly. "Forgive me, if I did any injustice to you." And he slowly closed his eyes and he never opened his eyes again. His body had been cool and stiff. He died.

Anuprerana was too young to understand death. She started to shout "grandfather, grandfather."

Anuksha was grieved very much by her father's death. Tears filled her eyes. He forgave her father for his injustice done to her.

— SEVENTEEN —

As Anuprerana grew up slowly she could understand everything. She could understand that her mother and father don't love each other. She knew her mother is unhappy with her father.

So Anuksha always told Putul Dutt that I know you hate me. But please don't abuse me in front of your daughter. She understands everything. It will harm her.

"Let her understand." Putul Dutt said. "Let her understand what type of woman you are."

Anuksha didn't say anything. She thought it was better to be dumb than making argument with him.

One morning Anuprerana found her mother crying in the kitchen. She could understand that her father had abused her. She sat beside her mother on the table.

"Don't cry, mother." Anuprerana said consoling her mother. She wiped her tears off. "When I will grow up to a young woman then I will give you all happiness of life, you have missed."

Anuksha nodded her head turning her face towards Anuprerana. Her daughter's consoling relieved her pains from the heart and gave peace to her mind.

Anuksha slowly closed her eyes and felt a profound joy and pride. She hugged her deeply and kissed her soft cheeks affectionately with motherly love. "You are true daughter of mine." She said.

That was a Monday. Putul Dutt went out for his business and Anuprerana went out to her school. Anuksha was alone at home. Then suddenly to Anuksha's surprise Anupam appeared there.

Anuksha felt as if someone had rubbed ointment on the wound of many years of her heart.

"Anupam," The name had great satisfaction for her. She had seen the man of her heart after a gap of many years whom she always wanted to see. But she was afraid if someone had noticed him to come to her home.

Anuksha hadn't heard any word from him since her marriage to Putul Dutt.

Anupam shot a soft look at Anuksha as he sat beside her. "You are still beautiful as I saw you many years ago before your marriage." Anupam said. "You haven't changed."

Anuksha lowered her eyes and had a soft smile on her lips.

"I thought you have forgotten me." Anupam said. "I thought I would never see you again."

Suddenly Anuksha's face was saddened.

"Don't say like this." Anuksha said. "How can I forget you?" You are the first man in my life. I always think of you. You are always in my heart"

"You are happily married?" Anupam asked. "I think your husband is very kind and loving. He takes so much care of you."

Anuksha felt that Anupam is piercing thorn into her body.

"My husband is a person who doesn't understand the value of a wife." Anuksha said. "I am not happy with this marriage."

Anupam asked no more.

Anuksha went to the kitchen and made tea for Anupam. She brought tea to the room along with snacks on a plate and gave to Anupam.

Before leaving Anuksha's home Anupam took Anuksha's phone number and promised to phone her and she also took his phone number.

Anuksha closed the door. She stood before the mirror and looked her image in the mirror and tried to judge how much she has changed. Dark circle appeared under her eyes. Long mental restlessness had given a roughness on the smooth skin of cheeks. Time had damaged her beautiful face before age.

Next day Putul Dutt made a plan to go to Delhi for a month for his business purpose. The news made Anuksha very glad. She wanted to be alone when Anupam would come. She wanted Putul Dutt out of home when Anupam would come.

Anuksha was waiting for Anupam's call. Every now and then she walked around the phone and looked at the phone when phone will ring. Then the phone started to ring. She was sure it was Anupam's call. She was excited. She picked up the receiver and began to talk. She told him that Putul Dutt had gone to Delhi for one month. She told him to come in the afternoon and he promised to come.

Anupam came in the afternoon as he promised her. Anuksha was overwhelmed. Her heart filled with joy and excitement as if she rediscovered her lost days again. With sudden tears of joy rushed to her eyes.

"I thought you are not coming." Anuksha said wiping her tears. "I was eagerly waiting for you."

Anupam looked at her with affectionate expression in his eyes. "I don't want to hurt you." He said. "When I gave you word that I would come in the afternoon then I didn't want to break my word."

Anuksha didn't speak anything for a moment. Excessive emotion almost stopped her breath.

Then she stared at Anupam, "you may think that I have forgotten you as because I had been married."

Anupam smiled.

"It is true that the time brings change to everyone's life." Anuksha said. "So it is not true that I will forget the man whom I love most in my life. You are always in my heart. Now I had been little older than I was before."

Anupam was silent.

"I had a dream to walk together hand in hand with you. But that had never happened." Anuksha said with a deep sigh.

There was a long silence between them.

Anupam gazed at Anuksha. "That day you told that you are not happy with this marriage then really it hurt me very much. He said. "You should try to change your husband."

"Putul Dutt will never change." Anuksha said. "He will continue to be a drunkard and abusive till the last day of his life."

Then Anupam slowly walked over to the window.

"Where is your daughter?" Anupam asked.

"She is playing in the neighborhood." Anuksha answered.

By then Anuprerana came running towards Anuksha. She slowly leaned into her mother's arms.

Anupam turned his look down at Anuprerana. "She is a nice looking girl." He said smiling.

"Anupam," Anuksha said. "She is my daughter Anuprerana."

"She is like you." Anupam said. She gave a beautiful smile looking at Anupam.

"I am like my mother." Little Anuprerana said smartly.

As Anupam and Anuksha were talking between them Anuprerana was playing.

After drinking tea Anupam went out to a nearest shop with Anuprerana and Anuksha stood on the doorway watching them walking down the road together. She felt very happy to see them together.

Anupam bought Anuprerana lots of Chocolates and returned.

Little Anuprerana was very much impressed by Anupam and she had made friendship with him very quickly. She climbed on his back and made him to play horse riding with her.

Anuksha watched them and laughed.

"She can mix with people very easily." Anuksha said.

"Truly your daughter is very smart." Anupam said. "Anyway I love her too much."

"I don't know what I would do without her." Anuksha said. "She is my life."

At night when daughter Anuprerana was asleep then Anuksha and Anupam went out. They walked to the nearby football ground.

It was a beautiful night. They were walking on the grass together hand in hand. After a few moments walking they sat down on the ground. Anuksha softly laid her head on Anupam's shoulder. It was a moonlit night. The moon was shining like a queen among the stars. The night was full of romance. Anupam drew her close with his two arms.

"Anuksha," Anupam asked. "Are you really happy?"

Anuksha was silent dropping her head down.

"Anuksha," Anupam asked again. "Are you really happy?"

Anuksha had a long sigh. "Anupam" she asked. "Do you think everyone is happy in this world?"

"Actually I didn't mean that." Anupam said. "I am not talking about everyone. I am particularly talking about you. Because I had seen a cloud of melancholy on your face since I had seen you that day."

"Now I have a daughter and she makes me happy." Anuksha said.

"I know you love her very much." Anupam said.

"No one in this world is to love me except her." Anuksha said.

"I also thought marriage means full of happiness and joy." Anuksha said. "But for me marriage had been full of affliction and melancholy. Marriage had proved totally fatal for me.

"I am so sorry." Anupam said.

How could she tell him that she had been already married twice? Anuprerana is from her second husband. How could she tell him that her marriage to first husband Pratim Dutt was a tragedy? Then another tragedy was waiting for her. One year after her marriage suddenly one night Pratim Dutt had a severe heart attack and he died? After that again she was forced by her father to marry his younger brother

Putul Dutt who was working as a manager in a private company in Bombay. She thought that he will be not like his elder brother at least he will understand his wife's feelings. But she was wrong. He was also a drunkard and abusive like his elder brother.

Sometimes she thought to reveal everything to Anupam but next moment she feared that if he knows everything then he will be hurt. She was terrified to think that.

They walked around the play ground in silence. The moonlights fell on the wet grasses of the ground and shone brightly.

"When will your husband return form Delhi?" Anupam asked.

"One month later." Anuksha answered.

"Why did you marry this man?" Anupam asked. "Why didn't you refuse though you know everything about the man?"

"My father forced me to marry him." Anuksha said. "I had no courage to go against my father's decision. Believe me, Anupam, only I married him physically but already my heart, soul and mind had married you many years ago."

Anupam stared into her face. There were excessive affections in her eyes. His arms could not stop from hugging her.

— EIGHTEEN —

The evening came down over the city like a cool shadow. The electric bulbs started to illuminate the city and made the every moment wonderful. The streets were still crowded and full of uproars like as usual.

After walking for a few minutes Anupam and Anuksha sat down at a culvert opposite to railway track.They were talking and looking at the people passed by them.

The sky was clear. The moon slowly appeared in the sky like a bright pearl and slowly brightened the whole sky. The stars were twinkling pleasantly.

"Look to the moon." Anuksha said suddenly. There was a little touch of romance in her tone. "How the moon is slowly growing brighter as if the moon's brightness is going to rule over the earth."

Anupam raised his head up and looked to the moon. "Yes." He shook his head.

"I also thought my life will shine like the bright moon but all in vain." Anuksha had a long sigh.

Anupam slowly drew her close. He glanced at her with an intention to appease and romantically.

Anuksha was silent. She slowly lowered her eyes. She slowly buried her face into his arms and put an arm around him.

They were silent.

Then suddenly a local train crossed the place breaking their silence blowing the horn awfully.

"Oh, God!" Anuksha said. She swiftly put her fingers into the ears. She kept her fingers putting into ears until the last compartment of the train disappeared from the place.

Anuksha took a deep breath taking her fingers away from the ears. "Really it is intolerable."

"Anupam laughed." I am accustomed with this." He said, "Because my home is very near to the railway station."

Anupam drew her close again. She slowly put her head on his shoulder.

"Anuksha," Anupam said. His voice was very calm. "Are you really happy?" He asked. "Please don't hide anything from me."

Anuksha didn't say anything. She dropped her head down. She wanted to answer but she stopped.

"Anuksha are you really happy?" He asked again.

Anuksha threw a look across the street. She had a long sigh.

"Anupam," Anuksha said. "Do you think everyone is happy in this world?" She asked.

"I think not." Anupam answered. "But I am not saying in that sense. I am not talking about everyone. I am talking about you."

Anuksha gave a dry smile.

"What is the use of words happiness and unhappiness for me?" She said. "I have a lovely daughter and she keeps me happy."

"I know you love her very much." Anupam said. "I know she keeps you happy. But I ask you. Are you really happy from inside?"

Anuksha smiled indifferently looking up to the sky.

"You have a daughter to love you." Anupam said with almost unmindfully but no one to love me in this world."

Anuksha had no word to say.

Then after a while she turned her eyes at Anupam. "You also marry someone and you will have a beautiful lovely daughter and she will love you." She said.

"Show me a woman I will marry?" Anupam asked. "Show me a woman who really loves me?"

There are so many women in this world." Anuksha said. "Marry one of them who love you."

"Find me a particular woman who really loves me? Who really understands me?" Anupam asked.

"You have to find out yourself." Anuksha answered.

"It is very tough to find out true love." Anupam said. "True love comes only once in life.It is like an illusion and devine grace of god. Only few are lucky to get the taste of true love.

— NINETEEN —

"I thought that marriage is a holy, full of happiness. But for me marriage had been a hell, full of sorrowness." Anuksha said.

Anupam softly held her hand. "Don't say like this." He said.

Anuksha glanced at him. There was rare kind fascination on his face. She was not ready to see such a fascination on his face.

Then Anupam slowly bent his head down and kissed her hand.

"You know Anuksha!" Anupam said. "Marriage" this word has meanings for some and for some this word is worthless.

They got out of the culvert and started walking towards home.

Anupam put his hand around her and started to walk down the street.

"A man is a weaker than a woman." Anupam said suddenly. "A man can't live without a woman but a woman can live without a man. A woman can alter her heart to a rock in time but a man can't."

Anuksha glanced at him. But he was looking across the last part of the corridor almost indifferently.

As they walked abruptly Anuksha stumbled on a table kept in the middle of the corridor. Anupam caught her hand and tried her to stand up.

It was a wild moment. Anuksha closed her eyes and tried to imagine making love with him wildly. She went back to her young days. She greatly felt a pleasure from inside as he held her tightly.

"You poor woman you can dream it. But reality is still away from your reach."

"Let's spend the night walking on the corridor." Anupam said.

Anuksha smiled. She stared up at him.

There was sudden change in the outside. The clean sky turned to cloudy. There were sudden flashes of lightning in the sky. Cold breeze started to blow heavily.

Abruptly light went out. They stood in the dark and held each other tightly.

"I have to leave you now." Anupam whispered.

"Spend the night here." Anuksha said.

"Not today." Anupam said.

"Why?" Anuksha said.

"No reason." Anupam answered.

Light returned to the home.

Anuksha stood on the door as Anupam walked out to the street.

"Good night." Anuksha waved her hand.

"Good night." Anupam said.

Anuksha shut the door. She went near the bed where her daughter was sleeping. Anuksha sat beside her daughter. She glanced down at her beautiful face.

Heavy rain started in the outside with storm. Rain drops fell on the roof with heavy sound.

Then Anuksha sat at the chair. She slowly leaned her back on the back of the chair and began to think about Anupam. How much she loved him. That was unimaginable. How much her life had been changed?

Anuksha thaught it would have been so exciting if she could marry Anupam. And it would have been more exciting if Anuprerana was her and his daughter.

Anuksha blamed her luck, what she thought that did not happen in her life.

— TWENTY —

Anuprerana always talked about Anupam. She called him "Good uncle." Anuksha was delighted.

Anuprerana took a great interest in Anupam as if she had blood relation with him.

Anupam brought lot of gifts and sweets mainly chocolates for her whenever he came to their home.

Anupam played with her. He took her for shopping. He took her to theatre. Some times he took her for long walk. He told beautiful stories and jokes to her and she was very much delighted. Every Saturday he accompanied her to her dancing class. He waited in the outside for her for hours to take her back to home.

Anupam loved Anuprerana in such a way as if she was his own daughter.

"Good uncle is such a great man mother." Anuprerana said. "If she was my father then I would have been so happy."

Anuksha didn't say anything. She mildly shook her head.

Anuprerana always asked so many questions about Anupam to her mother where she met him first. How did she meet him first? What did they talk between each other? Was there any third person who introduced them? How wonderful he looked when he was young? And so many questions she asked her. And Anuksha gave answer of all questions her daughter asked without any hesitation.

"Now you are a grown up girl." Anuksha said. "You should know everything. I don't want to hide anything from you. You are enough old to know what is right and what is wrong."

"So tell me about you and good uncle." Anuprerana said. "I am very excited and anxious to know about you and good uncle."

"Then listen." Anuksha said. "I loved him. He was the first man in my life many years before your father married me."

"Did you love him very much?" Anuksha asked.

"Yes, I loved him very much." Anuksha answered. "He also loved me very much."

"Where did you meet him first and how?" Anuprerana asked.

"I met him first in Darjeeling." Anuksha answered. "He came to teach me."

"Why didn't you marry him?" Anuprerana asked.

Anuksha was silent.

"Tell me mother, why didn't you marry him?"

"There is a long story why I couldn't marry him." Anuksha said. "I was very unlucky from my birth. I lost my mother. I mean your grandmother at the age of one and half years old. After that my life had been hell. My father I mean your grandfather was drunkard and abusive. He never loved me. Then one day Neena aunt took me along with her to Darjeeling against your grandfather's wish where she got me admission in the school where she worked as a teacher. I spent the days there happily as if I could breathe some fresh air after long years. I had lot of friend there. I was popular in the school among the teachers and friends. Everyone loved me. I did good result every year in the examination. Then one day Neena aunt arranged Anupam as a home tutor for me to teach science and math. She was in search of government job. He stayed at his maternal uncle's home. He was a science graduate from one of the best colleges of Calcutta. After he became my home tutor my results started improving more than before. He was very handsome then. Days passed. He never taught me professionally. He always taught me from his heart. He always thought me as his own. After he became my home tutor I started to do better result than before. He was very smart and handsome then. His smart personality always attracted me. One day I fell in his love almost unknowingly. In the afternoon we together went out for long walk. We spent long time in silence together. Beside the hill we spent the days happily. Then one day suddenly he got a job in Kuwait through an agent and he had to fly for Kuwait in hurry. He even did not find out time to meet me. He left a letter in my name in his maternal uncle's home before he left for Kuwait. When I received the letter from his maternal uncle's home then I was really hurt. I cried out."

Anuksha stopped for a while then she again started to tell that after I passed the 12th class examination successfully one day my father went to Neena aunt's home in Darjeeling and brought me back to Calcutta along with him.

My happy days disappeared from life. Gradually my father's health started to deteriorate day by day for consuming heavy wine. I had to look after him. So I gave up my study. My father started to think about my marriage. When I heard he had arranged a man of his age for me only for his self interest then I was shocked. I protested. He threatened to kill me if I refused to marry the man he had arranged. At last I was bound to marry him. The man started to show his real character that was hidden behind his mask. His real character came out from behind the mask he was wearing. He was a drunkard and abusive like your grandfather. I mean like my father. I was living a hellish life. I always wailed and prayed to almighty in silence. Whenever I thought about Anupam my distressed heart cried out for him. I could feel deeply the anguish of my heart. My heart wailed and said Anupam you come wherever you are and rescue me from all torments of this hell."

— TWENTY ONE —

"Don't weep mother." Anuprerana said. She hugged mother very affectionately. She tried to pacify her.

Anuprerana slowly raised her mother's face up and wiped her tears with her affectionate fingers. She consoled her.

"I had never seen happiness in my life." Anuksha said. "I am very unlucky, but I want to see you happy forever my child. I want a beautiful life for you where the sun will never set.

"Really you have suffered a lot." Anuprerana said. "My grandfather was not a man, not a father, he was a butcher. He had destroyed your beautiful life. I hate him."

Anuksha glanced at Anuprerana with swollen eyes. "Forget all those." She said. She tried to smile forcefully.

"Mother," Anuprerana said. "It would have been so nice if you married good uncle and I would have got a beautiful father who had been so loving and careful towards his wife and daughter."

"Yes." Anuksha shook her head. But alas, she patted her forehead.

"Mother," Anuprerana said almost like a little kid. "Tell good uncle to visit our home regularly. I like to play with him."

"I will tell." Anuksha nodded.

But how could she tell him to visit her home regularly without his husband's permission. How could she tell her husband that he loved him and he came to her life like a bright light so many years before him?

— TWENTY TWO —

Anuprerana was sixteen. She gradually understood everything almost anything. It was time for her to enjoy the merriments and the beautiful things of life.

Anuprerana wanted to celebrate her sixteenth birthday very nicely. There should be some music, dance and her intimate friends will join her. That should be little showy.

Anuprerana arranged a beautiful party. She invited her all intimate friends to the party. She wanted her good uncle anyhow to be present at her birthday party.

Anuprerana told her mother to phone Anupam immediately to come to her birthday party anyhow leaving his all works and tell him that if he doesnot come then she would never talk to him.

Anuksha laughed. She dialed Anupam's number and phoned him to come to Anuprerana's birthday party anyhow and he had given word that he must be present at Anuprerana's birthday party.

"Anuprerana," Anuksha called. "Your gooduncle has given word to be present at your party, now if you invite him yourself then it will be better and he will be happier because he loves you very much like a daughter." Anuksha said.

"Okay." Anuprerana said. "Give me the telephone."

"Good uncle." Anuprerana said. "Tomorrow is my sixteent birthday. You must come leaving all works. My birthday will be totally glamourless if you will not come. It is my heartiest request and invitation to you to be presents at my birthday party. Give me word that you must come."

"Okay, Okay." Anupam laughed. "I have given you word." He said. "I must be present at your birthday party."

"Thank you good uncle, thank you." Anuprerana said. "I will wait for you.

Next day in the evening Anupam came to Anuprerana's birthday party. He brought a big and costly birthday gift for her, a high power music system she desired from him. He looked around the room. The room was decorated with colourful balloons, ribbons and bulbs. The room looked bright and wonderful. He looked for Anuprerana; he saw her talking with her friends. She looked pretty in her new birthday dress as if she was an elf. The birthday dress nicely suited her young look.

Anuprerana was excited to see Anupam at her party.

"Good uncle." Anuprerana said running towards him. "I was waiting for you. I asked mother so many times about you."

Anupam smiled, "I gave you word that I must come to your birthday party and I have kept it." He said.

Anupam handed the big and costly birthday gift to Anuprerana's hands. "You like music." He said. "So it is for you."

"Oh, Good uncle," Anuprerana said almost excitedly. "You are great, you are great."

Anuprerana showed the gift to everyone and told that it is a gift from my good uncle. Then she introduced him with all her friends.

Anuprerana gave the gift to mother's hands and told her to keep the gift carefully. "Mother, it is a most special gift for me." She said.

"Mother, Mother." Anuprerana suddenly shouted. "You stand beside good uncle." I will take a photograph of both of you together.

Anuksha blushed.

Anuprerana was ready with her camera.

"Don't blush mother." Anuprerana said. The photograph will remain as a memory.

Anuprerana took a photograph together of mother and Anupam as they stood together side by side.

"It will be a memorable photograph of my life like a precious gift." Anuprerana said. "I will keep it with me forever."

— TWENTY THREE —

Putul Dutt never liked the growing interest of her daughter Anuprerana on Anupam. He always looked it anxiously. He didn't like Anupam. He couldn't tolerate him anymore. For him Anupam was the most scornful person of his life.

When Putul Dutt asked Anuksha about Anupam then she told her husband that Anupam was only a friend but he didn't believe it. He always looked at him with a kind of suspicion and hatred.

Putul Dutt looked at Anuksha with suspicious eyes. "Don't tell lie." He said. "I can understand everything. What you both mother and daughter are doing in my home."

Anuksha didn't want to say anything. Better she thought to keep her mouth shut.

Anuksha's discontented heart cried for Anupam every moment though she was married. She had husband and a beautiful daughter yet she felt lonely. She always wanted to find her lost happiness on him. She had a belief that he was the only person who can give her meaningful happiness of a life.

Anupam was also a lonely man, no one to look after him no one to take care of him, no one to share his feelings and emotions.

Anuksha's past days were like some nightmares. She tried to forget them but she couldn't as if they always haunted he

At 6 O'clock in the evening Anupam arrived Anuksha's home. Anuprerana's little heart was filled with joy as she saw Anupam.

"Good uncle." With sudden Anuprerana shouted. There was wonderful joy in her tone. "Believe me I was thinking about you."

"Get ready quickly." Anupam said. "We will go for a long evening walk."

"Okay." Anuprerana said. "Wait just a minute. I will get ready within a minute."

Anuprerana quickly got ready and she was ready to go out for a long walk with Anupam.

They went out to the street as Anuksha looked on at them through the window and her heart filled with joy.

They started walking in the street almost like father and daughter.

Evening was wonderful. Evening cool wind brought some relief to the people from the hot of the day. Everywhere the lights were illuminating around. As they were walking Anupam started to tell beautiful stories to Anuprerana. Amid the stories he told some small jokes and she burst out laughing.

"Good uncle." Anuprerana said. "Tell me more jokes.I like your jokes very much. Really you know so many beautiful jokes no one can escape without laughing. Truly you are a joke master."

"Remember when your mind is upset then a joke can delight your mind." Anupam said.

"You are right good uncle." Anuprerana said. "I often tell mother to read some jokes when her mind is upset."

They walked into an ice cream parlour. They bought two ice creams and started walking again eating ice cream.

"Good uncle." Anuprerana suddenly asked. "Why are you still unmarried?"

"Because I still haven't found the right woman," Anupam answered after silence of a moment.

"There are so many women in this world." Anuprerana said. "You can chose anyone and you can marry."

Anupam laughed. "You don't understand now," He said. When you will grow up to a young lady then you will understand."

"Good uncle if I ask you one question would you mind? Anuprerana asked.

"Why should I mind?" Anupam answered. "You can ask me any question."

"How did you meet my mother first?" Anuprerana asked.

"That is a long story." Anupam answered.

"Mother had told me everything." Anuprerana said.

"What had your mother told?" Anupam asked.

"How and where did you meet my mother first," Anuprerana answered.

"And what had your mother told you, Anuprerana?" Anupam asked.

"So many things about you," Anuprerana quickly answered.

They were walking silently then Anupam turned his eyes at Anuprerana. "Let's go back home." He said. "I think your mother is waiting for you."

"Okay, let's go back." Anuprerana nodded. She grabbed his hand.

When they came back home they foundAnuksha standing near the window looking out to the street.

"Mother," Anuprerana said. "You are still standing near the window."

Anuksha smiled softly. "I am getting bored at home alone, so I am looking at the people in the street to kill my boredom. Also I was waiting for you to come."

"Good uncle told me so many beautiful stories and jokes." Anuprerana said. "Those stories and jokes were so delightfull and funny."

"I think you have enjoyed so much." Anuksha said.

"Yes, mother," Anuprerana answered. "I have enjoyed so much."

"You talk with Anupam." Anuksha said. "I am going to make tea for him."

"No need to make tea for me." Anupam said. "Better you give me a glass of cold water."

Anuksha walked into the kitchen and came back with a glass of cold water and handed the glass to Anupam's hand. Anupam looked up at Anuksha's face and smiled as he took the glass from her hand.

Anuprerana left them alone and went to her room for study.

Anuksha always tried to find out a sweet and holy relationship between Anupam and her daughter Anuprerana. She always thought them as father and daughter. She always thought Anupam as her father. Anupam had such a great personality to make everyone his own. Anuksha was overwhelmed.

"You have got a nice daughter Anuksha." Anupam always said. "She is so nice."

"She is like you." Anuksha said with a smile. "She loves you too much."

"Actually I don't know why she had mixed with me very easily." Anupam said. "Sometimes I think I had any relationship with her in my previous birth."

"Anupam," Anuksha said. Her voice was smooth. "I have a request to you."

"Tell me what your request is?" Anupam asked with wonder in his eyes.

"We all three will eat supper together." Anuksha answered.

"Any special dish"? Anupam asked funnily.

"Your favourite fish curry," Anuksha laughed. "I am cooking specially for you."

"Then I will eat." Anupam said funnily.

They enjoyed supper together on the dining table like a very happy family. The special dish Anuksha cooked for Anupam was delicious and he praised her cooking.

After supper Anupam and Anuksha went out as Anuprerana was busy watching Television.

Anuksha softly held Anupam's hand. Her body was thrilled with an unknown fear and joy. Next moment she thought that she was a mother of a young daughter. If anybody looked them then it was a matter a shame.

They walked looking around. They suddenly looked up to the sky and tried to count the stars and laughed like two small kids almost falling over each other.

"My life is like a rock where there is no any savor." Suddenly Anupam said.

Anuksha slowly looked at Anupam. "Why do you say like this?" She said. Don't say like this. It hurts me."

As they walked with sudden Anuksha stumbled over a high speed breaker. She got ach on the knee.

"Are you Okay?" Anupam asked.

"Yes." Anuksha shook her head.

Anupam held out his hand to her. As she held his hand he quickly bent over her and helped her to stand. "Be careful." He said.

"We not only should be careful on the street of the city but also we should be careful on the street of life." Anuksha said almost philosophically.

"You are talking like a philosopher." Anupam said throwing a soft look at her.

Then suddenly Anupam noticed that she could not walk perfectly, she was walking like a lame. Anupam went to a nearby Medicine shop and bought an ointment. He squeezed out little ointment from the tube and applied on the knee. Then he affectionately massaged the knee. After massege for some minutes she got relief from the pain. She was okay now and she could walk perfectly.

With sudden there was a beautiful expression of young love on Anuksha's face. Her mind flew back to the days she spent with Anupam. Her memories with Anupam were still young and alive in her mind. Her mind was missing for the moment in the garden of those memories.

"I have loved only one woman in my life that was you." Anupam said. "I never thought or dreamt of any other woman. If I think or dream any other woman then it will be a sin."

"I also loved one man that is you." Anuksha said. "I love you with all my heart. I was married to two men whom I never loved. But my luck was very bad. My luck betrayed me. I was compelled to marry the men I never loved. I always wanted to marry the man I loved but that never happened. Now my life is like a sinking boat."

Anupam took her hand. A pleasant feeling touched her soul. She looked at him. He was little unmindful.

Then abruptly electricity went out. The city sank into the sea of darkness. "Let's go back." Anuksha said. "Anuprerana is alone at home. She will be afraid."

"Okay." Anupam said.

Anuksha often wondered why she married the men she never loved? Why she couldn't gather courage within her to oppose her father? Why she couldn't marry Anupam whom she loved whole heartedly? She was puzzled by many questions. A pain escaped through her heart that was like a sharp knife.

Anuksha thought she had spent half of her life in sorrow and pain. She married but she never got the happiness of married life. Only some bitterness had devoured her married life.

Anuksha could not sleep. Her mind was restless. She felt almost suffocated. Sudden impulse weakened her. When Anuksha's daughter slept then she slowly got out of the bed. The room was silent and dark. She walked over to the window. She opened one part of the window and pulled up the curtain and allowed fresh air to enter inside. She felt relaxed. She stood near the window looking out. Again her mind flew back to the past world where she and Anupam once spent many memorable moments of life. She started to walk through the lane of memories and thought many things about herself and Anupam.

— TWENTY FOUR —

Putul Dutt sat at the dining table along with Anupam. Though he didn't like his presence at the dining table but he didn't object. He was silent.

Then Anuprerana came to the dining table. She sat beside Anupam and gave him company at the dining table. Putul Dutt raised his head. He slowly turned around and looked at her daughter Anuprerana cynically. "You are also like your mother." He mumbled.

After dinner Anuksha and Anuprerana went off to the dressing room. Anuksha threw a look to the mirror.

"How I look, Anuprerana?" Anuksha asked.

Anuprerana laughed. "Mother you look beautiful and younger than your age. Don't be upset about your look. You are still beautiful you were." She said.

Anuksha felt proud.

Anuprerana stood beside mother. She hugged her mother excitedly in joy. "Mother truly you look younger than your age."

Anuksha was glad to hear such a beautiful word from her daughter.

"Mother," Anuprerana said. "Good uncle is such a nice man. He talks lots about you."

Anuksha blushed.

They sat on the bed together like two friends.

Anuprerana slowly laid her head on mother's shoulder. "I think you would have been so happy in life if you married Good uncle." She said. "He would have given you everything; loves, affection, joy, happiness. He would have taken more care about you."

Anuksha was silent. She had no word to tell her daughter.

"Good uncle told me that you were brilliant student in the class. You brain could catch everything very easily. He also said that you were so beautiful when you were young. He said that I have got your beauty."

Anuksha was silent.

"You are the only woman Good uncle had admired in life." Anuksha said.

Anuksha was still silent.

"Mother," Anuprerana asked. "Good uncle is a well established man but still he is unmarried why?"

"Perhaps he still hadn't found the right woman he desired." Anuksha answered.

Anupam entered into the drawing room, "Sorry." He said politely. "I think I have disturbed."

"No." Anuksha said.

"Good uncle." Anuprerana said. "You have longevity. Actually we were talking about you."

"I have come here to say you both good bye." Anupam said smiling.

"Good uncle you must come tomorrow and we will have a dinner together like today," Anuprerana said.

"Okay, Okay." Anupam laughed. "If I don't have any work then I must come." Anupam said and left.

Windows were open, winds struck the curtains and made them to wave up and down. Anuksha slowly left her back on the sofa and started to think something seriously.

By then Putul Dutt came in. He stood in front of her. He looked down at her. His look contained anger.

"You didn't expect me here?" Putul Dutt said. His tone was full of jealousness and pinching.

Anuksha felt very angry. She didn't say anything for a moment. "Why are you saying like this?" She asked.

Putul Dutt didn't say any word. Only he laughed like a half mad.

Putul Dutt sat by her side. He slowly turned his eyes at her. "Anupam is a nice fellow?" He said willingly. "Once upon a time he was a good friend of you and still he is a good friend of you." He laughed again. "I know a good friend is for forever. He never likes me with you." He laughed again but then continuously for a minute.

Anuksha was almost dumb. She was looking to another side.

Putul Dutt quickly put a cigarette into lips and lit it. He puffed almost unmindfully.

"I know you had never enjoyed happiness after your marriage with me." Putul Dutt said blowing smokes through the nostrils. "You should have it in your luck."

"Am I right?" Putul Dutt asked.

"I don't know." Anuksha answered.

Then as she started to go out of the room Putul Dutt caught her hand. "Where are you going?" He asked with a notorious smile. You sit beside me. I have lot of question to ask you and you have to answer."

"Please let me go." Anuksha said trying to free her hand. "I am sleepy."

"Forget your sleep." Putul Dutt said.

"Listen." Putul Dutt said. "Do you think I don't know anything about you and that bustard? Do you think I am a fool? His voice was full of anger. He threw the half burned cigeratte out of window harshly."

"What are you saying all these?" Anuksha said. She tried to free her hand again from his grip but she could not. His grip was very firm.

"You know very well what I am saying all these." Putul Dutt answered. "Don't pretend as if you don't understand anything."

"What rubbish you are saying about all these, I don't understand." Anuksha said.

Putul Dutt had a sudden laugh. "You know very well my lovely wife, you know very well." He said. He suddenly squeezed her hand. "Your dear friend was the first man I mean first love in your life."

"Yes, he is my friend." Anuksha said. "I met him first when I was young. He is a good friend of mine and nothing."

"Don't try to make me fool." Putul Dutt said. "I know you would have married him."

"Please stop all these bogus talking." Anuksha said almost angrily. "Please leave me now. I have so many works to do. I have no time for your bogus talkings."

"You are crazy of love." Putul Dutt said. "My darling, you are a dirty woman. Remember you are a mother of a young daughter. Keep yourself away from all these dirty things. Otherwise people will spit on you."

Anuksha bit her lips in anger. Her whole body started trembling in anger. But she controlled her anger. She thought. What is the use of going to any argument with him? Rather she preferred to be silent.

But Putul Dutt continued to scold her meaninglessly. "I know why you forced me to keep your daughter's name Anuprerana." He said, because that bastard's name also starts with 'A'."

"My name also starts with 'A'." Anuksha said.

Putul Dutt was silent.

"Remember." Anuksha said. "I am your wife and you should behave me like your wife. You shouldn't blame me falsely."

"I know how to behave with you." Putul Dutt said. "You are a woman to be behaved like this. You deserve this kind of behaviour from your husband because you are not a good woman. I think myself very unlucky to marry you."

"I think I am very unlucky to marry a person like you." Anuksha said.

"Really," Putul Dutt laughed. "You are very unlucky to marry a person like me. You had married me and you had been away from love and affection. Now he has come to offer you love and affection and everything you expected from a man." He laughed again.

Anuksha was almost dumb. She had no word to tell. She felt her blood circulation was running very fast.

"You may think how I have come to know about all these." Putul Dutt said with a light smile. "When a woman falls in love then an abnormality is seen in her behaviour and I have seen that abnormality in you. You are a woman of licentious character."

Anuksha couldn't bear all those anymore. "You will never change." She said and went out of the room. She was almost suffocated by her husband's indigestible words. She started breathing fast.

There was always hatred to her husband from the beginning but now it has been more and more prominent due to his dirty and suspicious behaviour towards her. Her life had been full of bitterness. She wanted to run away from bitterness of life. Only one man could solace her from bitterness of life, he was Anupam. Day by day her mind went away from her husband and came closer to Anupam.

In the midnight when all fell asleep then Anuksha silently opened the door and went out to the veranda. She slowly left her tired body into the arm chair.

As Anuksha slowly closed her strained eyes suddenly there were thunders and lightning in the sky. A few seconds later the rain had begun to drop in roaring sound.

Anuksha wanted to run out to the street to wash out her all sorrowness and pains of heart in the rain water.She wanted to lighten her body and soul.

Anuksha thought of Anupam. Anupam's amiable face floated before her eyes. She felt as if he was standing beside her. She felt protective and satisfaction. Her body was thrilled with sudden pleasure. She slowly shut her eyes. She could feel the warmth of his two arms around her. Feeling was so wonderful as if she was living in the heaven of pleasure.

"Anupam, Anupam." Anuksha suddenly shouted out.

There was only a cry in her thirsty heart to hug him wholeheartedly. Tears slowly dampened her indifferent eyes. Tears came down like some small river streams on her face to slake her dry skin.

Rain continued and there were small and big thunders and lightnings in different corners of the sky. Anuksha slowly opened her eyes. She wiped her tears off with the back of hand. She got off the arm chair and slowly walked inside closing the door. She went to her room and lay on the bed. She was awoke whole night. The memories violently disturbed her.

— TWENTY FIVE —

Anuksha noticed old curtains had been fade so she altered the old curtains from the windows. The new curtains had brought glow not only to the windows but also to the whole room.

She stood near the window of the drawing room looking out at Anupam and Anuprerana talking and laughing on a funny topic near the entrance gate. She felt very glad. She thought perhaps they were daughter and father in the pre birth.

How much Anuprerana talking about Anupam she never talked about her own father. She loved him very much. He was an ideal person for her. She always wanted to be like him. She always praised his vision about woman. He says a woman has great importance to build a healthy society.

As Anuprerana saw her mother she almost shouted excitedly. "Mother," she said. "Good uncle will stay at our home at night."

Anuksha had a soft smile at her daughter.

"Anuprerana," Anuksha said to herself. "You are very lucky. You have got fatherly love from a man who is not your father. You are very lucky you have got fatherly love from a man whom I loved but I am very unlucky I couldn't marry him."

"Mother." Anuprerana suddenly asked. "Are you Okay?" She softly put her arm around her neck.

"I am Okay." Anuksha answered.

"I think you are tired, mother." Anuprerana said. "Now you need some rest. So you directly go to the bed.

"I am quite Okay, my daughter." Anuksha said. "You no need to be worry about me." Now you go and do your study.

It was about midnight. Anuksha was still awake. She had no sleep. Her mind was heavy with different thoughts.

Anuksha got out of the bed. She walked over to the window. She opened the window. It was almost silent in the outside. Gentle wind struck her face and left a cool feeling of December on her body.

Anuksha shut the window and went back to the bed. She pulled a blanket over her head and tried to sleep closing eyes. A few seconds later she fell into asleep.

Anuksha began dreaming. She found herself sitting in a park. Anupam came walking over the grasses across her and stood silently behind her. But she was not aware of his presence. Then as Anupam stood in front of her she was almost thrilled and nervous. She couldn't raise her head. Their eyes met. He lowered himself over her and took her face in between his two palms.

Anuksha stood and held Anupam's hand. They started walking on the grasses in silence. Then a few minutes later he suddenly disappeared into the silent darkness of the night leaving her alone in the park.

Anuksha woke up in the morning with a deep feeling of the dream.

"Mother," Anuprerana asked. "Are you okay now?"

"Yes." Anuksha smiled and answered "I am totally okay now." She softly kissed her daughter.

Anuksha had a hurried glance up at the wall clock. "Oh God!" She said to herself. "It is 9 O'clock. I am too late to get up. Has your father gone out?" She asked.

"Yes, father has gone out about one hour ago." Anuprerana answered. He asked me about you. I have told him that you are not well."

"Has he eaten breakfast?" Anuksha asked.

"Yes," Anuprerana answered. "He has eaten breakfast. I have given him toasted breads and omlet with a cup of hot tea."

"Have you eaten your breakfast?" Anuksha asked.

"You no need to think for me." Anuprerana answered swiftly. Now you go to the bathroom and wash your face and drink hot cup of tea. I am going to the kitchen to make tea for you. You will taste how I make tea."

Anuksha looked at Anuprerana almost affectionately. "How long will you take care of me?" She asked. "When you will get married then you will forget me."

"No mother." Anuprerana said. "I will never get married." She hugged her mother. "I will never forget you. You will be always within my heart."

"Everyone says that." Anuksha said smiling.

"No." Anuprerana said. "I am not like others."

"Time will say." Anuksha said and went over to the basin to wash her face.

As Anuksha wiped her face Anuprerana handed over the hot cup of tea to her hand.

Anuksha gently gave a mild sip into the tea. "Wonderful." She nodded her head. My daughter is a very good tea maker. She had a smile on her face.

"Don't tease me, mother, Please." Anuprerana said with a childish like gesture.

"I am not teasing you my daughter." Anuksha said. "I am praising you."

"Thank you." Anuprerana said. "Mother now I will go out for shopping with good uncle. He is waiting for me at the shopping center."

"Okay." Anuksha said. "You will come soon."

"Okay, mother." Anuprerana said.

Anuprerana hurriedly got dressed and went out waving her hand at mother.

Then Putul Dutta came home. He went directly into Anuksha's room. He looked at her very strangely that made her almost wonder.

"Why does that bastard Anupam often come to my home?" Putul Dutt asked in a harsh tone.

"He comes only for Anuprerana." Anuksha answered calmly. "He loves her as his daughter."

"Oh. I see." Putul Dutt shook his head with a mimic expression on his face. "He loves Anuprerana like his daughter. Don't try to make me fool." Suddenly he became angry. I know everything. Both you are playing a game using my daughter as a shield.

"Don't say like this." Anuksha said. "We are not playing any game. If you don't like then tell him not to come to your home."

"Why should I tell him?" Putul Dutt said in anger. "You should tell him because you invited him to my home not I."

"I can't tell." Anuksha said. "I don't see anything wrong on him. He is a good person."

"Remember." Putul Dutt shouted violently. "I am your husband. I have a prestige and don't spoil my prestige. If you want to play a love game then you will play it after my death. Then no one will remain to tell you. Then you can do anything you like. No one will hinder you."

"You are blaming me without any truth." Anuksha said. "Don't stick any false allegation on my character. It is true that he was my friend and still he is my friend."

"Friend"! Putul Dutta muttered. "I will kill that bastered. You don't know my anger. I will drink his blood." He quickly lit a cigarette and walked out of the room slamming the door behind him.

— TWENTY SIX —

Anuprerana passed the twelve class examination very successfully with distinction. But her mother Anuksha was not in a mood to celebrate her daughter's success because she had a quarrel in the morning with her father. He was jealous of her all the time. He never liked to see her happy as if he was adamant about that.

Anupam was overwhelmed to hear Anuprerana's result. But her own father was not overwhelmed by her success. He was busy drinking wine from the morning after he went out from the home quarreling with Anuksha. Anupam came to her home to congratulate her with lots of gifts and sweets for her. He gave her a gold plated wrist watch as he promised her.

"Congratulation Anuprerana," Anupam said. "I am really very happy, Anuprerana, You can't imagine."

"Good uncle, I know you will be happy. So I have given you the news first." Anuprerana said. You are a great well wisher of mine.

Anupam smiled. "Do you like the wrist watch?" He asked.

"Oh, beautiful," Anuprerana shouted excitedly widening her eyes. She quickly put on the wrist watch into her hand and showed to Anupam smiling pleasantly.

"Open that box." Anupam said pointing at the dress box.

Anuprerana opened the box and brought out the blue yellow dress.It was a golden fabric salwar. She went into the bedroom and put on the new dress. She stood before the mirror and looked her image in the mirror. She looked beautiful in her new dress. The new dress fitted in her slim body nicely.

"You are looking beautiful in your new dress." Anupam said. "The colour is matching you nicely."

"Good uncle," Anuprerana said. You are really great, you know my choice.

As Anuksha came in Anupam glanced at her.

"Today is the joyful day for you." Anupam said. "Your daughter had performed a good result."

Anuksha slowly shook her head. It is her hard work and your inspiration.

"You should celebrate the day with great pleasure and happiness." Anupam said.

"Happiness is not written in my life." Anuksha said indifferently.

"Don't say like this." Anupam said. He glanced into her eyes. What has happened to you? Anupam asked. "You look upset."

"Nothing," Anuksha answered softly.

"Don't you like me to come to your home?" Anupam asked.

Anuksha quickly turned her eyes at Anupam. "Who has told you that I don't like you to come to my home?" She asked.

"No one," Anupam muttered. "I have seen a sudden change in you." He said, you are talking very little with me today as if you are trying to avoid me."

Anuksha smiled. "Don't blame me like this." She said. Actually I donot know why my mind is upset today."

Forget all those.Anupam said. "Are you inviting anyone to celebrate your daughter's success?" Anupam asked.

"No." Anuksha answered. Neither I have invited anyone nor have I told anyone personally about her result. You are the first person she has informed about her result."

"Truly I am very happy to hear her result." Anupam said. "She is very brilliant. I want her great success in the coming days."

"You know Anupam." Anuksha said. "She loves you too much like father. I think she is also very lucky to here a person like you. It is a great blessing of god to her."

"I also love her too much like a daughter though I am unmarried. I have no daughter." Anupam said.

By then Putul Dutt arrived home. He was drunk. He looked at both Anupam and Anuksha ferociously. He muttered something indistinctively.

"Anuksha," Mr. Putul Dutt shouted as he walked into his room.

Anuksha didn't give any reply.

"Anuksha," Mr Putul Dutt shouted again now violently.

"You wait just a minute." Anuksha told Anupam. And she went to Putul Dutt's room to enquire why he is calling her.

Mr. Putul Dutta looked at Anuksha. There were lots of angers in his look. "Why this bastard is at my home?" He asked. "You don't know that I hate him?"

"Please don't create a chaos today." Anuksha pleaded him. "Today is the day of joy and celebration. Your daughter has done a successful result. But you have not brought a single gift for her. Even you haven't congratulated her. I hate you to tell as a father of Anuprerana.

"Don't try to hide your fault. Don't try to use your daughter as a shield." Putul Dutt said.

Anuksha didn't say anything. She silently came out of the room. She went to the kitchen and turned on the oven with a gas lighter and started to cook meal for husband Putul Dutt.

Some friend of Anuprerana visited her to congratulate. She was excited.

Anuprerana went into the kitchen. "What are you cooking mother?" She asked. Some friends have come. Please arrange sweets for them.

"Don't think for that." Anuksha said. "Now you go and give company to your friends. Let me finish cooking for your father first then I will arrange sweets for them."

"Father has gone out puffing a cigarette." Anuprerana said.He looked angry.

"Where"? Anuksha asked.

"Don't know." Anuprerana answered. "He didn't say me anything."

"Damn your father." Anuksha muttered. "Your father can't be counted in the category of human being. He is an animal. He has given me only suffering whole life."

"You know his nature, mother." Anuprerana consoled her mother. "Don't be upset."

"Okay." Anuksha said taking a deep sigh. "Now you go and give company to your friend. I am arranging sweets for your friends."

Anuprerana was wild with excitement. She turned on the music and started to dance with her friends as Anupam looked on.

"Good uncle." Anuprerana shouted. "Come and join us."

"No thanks." Anupam smiled. "You dance. I am enjoying your dance."

Anuksha brought sweets and creamy cakes on a tray to the room for all.

All the friends cheered up in excitement. They stopped dancing and sat down on the table to eat sweets and creamy cakes.

"Delicious as your success, Anuprerana," One of Anuprerana's friends said.

"Yes." Other friend also joined her.

Anuprerana laughed. "Don't make me shame."

"All of you bless Anuprerana for a better future." Anuksha said.

"Aunt, don't worry." All friends of Anuprerana said. "Our blessings are always with her. She is our best friend. We hope to eat such delicious sweets and cake every year."

"All of you enjoy." Anuksha said and walked out of the room with the tray on hand.

Anupam got out of the chair and followed her into the kitchen. "Where is your husband?" He asked Anuksha.

"He has just gone out to somewhere." Anuksha answered.

"I think your husband has been very angry to see me here." Anupam said.

"Let him be angry." Anuksha said calmly. "He will burn himself in the fire of his own anger. I don't care now. I had been habituated with all these."

When all the friends of Anuprerana had left then the house had been silent as before.

Anuprerana walked over to her mother. She sat beside her mother and slowly laid her head over her mother's shoulder.

"Mother," Anuprerana said softly. "Good uncle is a wonderful person. He can share joy and sorrowness of others.Ithink he finds happiness there."

Anuksha was silent. She softly placed her hand on Anuprerana's head. "Truly he is a wonderful person." She said.

"I know, he loves you too much." Anuprerana said. "He can feel your pains. He can understand you inner feelings. I think no one understands you better than him."

Anuksha didn't say anything.

"Sometimes I think if he was your husband and my father then truly life would have been so wonderful."

All of sudden two drops of tear shone in Anuksha's eyes. She quickly wiped her tears with the back of her hand.

Anuksha slowly ran her fingers through Anuprerana's hairs and thinking something deeply.

"Your marriage to my father was really a mournful event in your life." Anuprerana said. "You have never seen a single drop of happiness in your life. Truly it is very sad."

Anuksha wept silently. "I love you so much my daughter. I love you so much." She hugged her deeply. "I am really very fortunate. I am the happiest mother in the world who has got such a wonderful daughter like you, who can understand mother's feelings who wants to see her mother always happy. Lots of thank to god."

"Don't weep mother." Anuprerana wiped Anuksha's tears very lovingly. "Almighty will open his eyes one day."

Anuprerana looked at her mother's face. Her face has been pale and eyes were swollen.

"Good uncle always talks about you." Anuprerana said.

"What he talks about me?" Anuksha asked pleasently.

"He talks so many sweet things about you." Anuprerana answered. "How he met you, how he expressed his love to you, you were so slim and beautiful when you were young. He often took you for long walk and shared so many words with you."

Suddenly Anuksha went back to her past days she spent with Anupam for the moment. So many sweet events were stored in her memory box. She opened the box and brought out them. She played with them and forgot all her pains of life for some moments. It delighted and slaked her thirst.

— TWENTY SEVEN —

At night when Anuprerana and her father fell into deep sleep then Anuksha opened the door and silently went out to the street where Anupam was waiting for her.

They held each other's hands and walked down the illuminating street talking and gossiping. They were very glad. They felt free like new freedom.

"Do you remember those beautiful days?" Anupam asked.

"Not once, million times." Anuksha answered pleasantly.

They were passing by a newly constructed residential complex.

The different flowers were in full bloom. The wind brought multi fragrances of the flowers to their nostrils.

Anuksha slowly shut her eyes, and deeply inhaled the fragrance. "Oh very sweet," She uttered.

Anupam turned his look at Anuksha. She was still shutting her eyes.

Anupam smiled. "Does Anuprerana understand everything?" Anupam asked.

"She is enough old to understand." Anuksha answered. "After all she is my daughter and she loves me from heart."

"Sometimes I think she is my daughter." Anupam said without any hesitation.

"She loves you very much." Anuksha said.

Anuksha suddenly looked back. "We have come a long way. Suddenly fear struck her if someone noticed them.

"We should go back home." Anuksha said.

"Okay." Anupam shook his head.

"Let me accompany you up to your home."

Anupam grabbed her hand and started walking towards her home. There was a long silence in between them like a third person walking with them.

Her heart cried out as she left him near the door. She wanted to run away with him but she was chained in a prison of social usage. She was helpless because she was still a wife of someone.

The night passed very quickly.

"I think you had enjoyed too much yesterday." Anuksha asked Anuprerana as she got up in the morning.

"Yes mother." Anuprerana smiled. "Mother," she asked. "Will good uncle come today?"

"I don't know." Anuksha answered. She threw a long look at her then she asked her do you love him very much?

"Yes I love him very much." Anuprerana said very proudly. "Why, Don't you love him mother?" She hugged mother deeply.

Anuksha blushed. She gave a soft kiss on her forehead.

"Good uncle promised to take me to the theatre today." Anuprerana said.

"Then he may come." Anuksha said.

In the afternoon Anupam came as he gave word to Anuprerana. "Get ready quickly, Anuprerana." He said. "I will take you to the theater. A beautiful film is being shown and today is the last day so we should go in hurry otherwise it will be difficult to get ticket."

"Okay, I am getting ready within a minute." Anuprerana said very pleasantly and ran into her room and started to get dressed.

"Anuprerana asked me about you in the morning." Anuksha said smiling.

"I gave her word yesterday that I would take her to theatre. Then how can I miss it? If I don't come then it will be a great injustice to her." Anupam said swiftly in a fun mixing tone.

"Really she is mad of you." Anuksha gave a laugh.

"Your daughter is growing very pretty." Anupam said. "She is very intelligent. You should be proud of her."

"I am really proud of her." Anuksha said. "We are like two friends. We discuss everything between each other. We don't hide anything from each other."

"Now she is enough old to understand everything." Anupam said.

Anuprerana was already ready. "I am ready, Good uncle." She said twisting her body on the floor. She threw a smiling looking across Anupam.

Anupam looked at her. "Then let us go." He said.

"Bye, mother," Anuprerana said and went out holding his hand as Anuksha looked on at them very proudly.

Bye, she waved her hand. She looked across them leaning her head against the door frame.

It was about ten O'clock when Anupam and Anuprerana returned from theater. She was tired. She already ate meal in a restaurant so she didn't eat meal at night and directly went to the bed and fell into a deep sleep.

Anupam didn't go to his home. He was waiting for Anuksha in the outside.

"Wait, Anupam." Anuksha said. She looked around and silently went out closing the door.

"It was a starry night without the moon. The wind was gentle. There was aroma of romance in the air.

"It is a beautiful night." Anupam said, "There was spark of romance in his voice.

"Yes." Anuksha shook her head slowly. She was almost excited.

Anupam slowly turned around and glanced at Anuksha. "You look too younger today." He said in a soft voice. He mildly squeezed her wrist.

Anuksha smiled blushing. She felt little haughty.

"Anuksha," Anupam said, Emotion engulfed his voice. "Thousand dreams are hatched within us as we can give some of them a touch of reality. Most of them are left orphan. We slaughter most of them like butchers."

"You are right, Anupam." Anuksha said. "What can we do? We are helpless. We are like two helpless dolls in the hand of destiny."

Anupam was silent for a long time as if he followed the silence. Then he turned his eyes at Anuksha. "You are right." He said calmly. "But all the times we shouldn't blame destiny."

"Dreams are some inevitable companions of life." Anuksha said. "They are sweet companions of sorrow and happiness of life. We can't avoid them"

"But we don't know how to honour them." Anupam said sadly.

Suddenly they saw the light of head lights of a car coming towards them. They hurriedly hid themselves behind a wall.

As the car went away they came out from behind the wall looking around very carefully and timidly almost like two thieves.

"Let's spend the night on the street." Anupam said giving a smiling look at Anuksha.

"Anuksha had a laugh. "Time and fear willn't permit us."

"Your husband will kill both of us if he sees us now together." He laughed.

"Truly I am too much afraid of him." Anuksha said.

Abruptly Anuksha looked very serious.

Anupam glanced at Anuksha. "What are you thinking Anuksha?" He asked.

"Future," Anuksha mumbled indistinctively.

"Future?" There was enough wonder in his voice.

"I haven't seen any light in the path of future." Anuksha said unmindfully.

"Believe me." Anupam said. "I have seen a beautiful light in the path of your future. Your daughter will show you a light in the path of your future. Your future will be brighter than your past."

A long silence surrounded Anuksha like a shawl.

"Anuksha," Anupam said. "I have loved only one woman in life that is you and I want to honour your love."

Anuksha had no word to express. Only two drops of sudden tear dampened her eyes.

"Anuksha," Anupam said. "When I saw you first at Neena aunt's home then you were too young and jolly. Now you are a mother of a young daughter. But still I find that youthness in you except your jolliness. It is true that marriage brings so many changes to a woman's life physically and mentally and it is also true that a marriage brings more and more jolliness to life."

"Don't think me wrong, Anupam," Anuksha said. "I still love you, Anupam. I still admire you as the ideal man in my life as I admired you many years ago."

Anupam didn't say anything. He walked slowly and silently.

Anuksha slowly stared at Anupam. "Don't hurt my heart." She softly said. "Already I had been broken. Don't break me anymore."

"I have no any desire to hurt you," Anupam said. "I always want to see you happy and glad."

"You know, Anupam." Anuksha said. She took a deep sigh. "I have suffered the bitterness of life before time as if I deserved it."

"You have suffered the bitter experience of life." Anupam said. "But your good days are ahead. You must taste the sweet experience of life. Your daughter will bring the fountains of joy and happiness to your life."

A deep feeling hugged them like an arm.

"Don't lose the battle of life." Anupam encouraged Anuksha. "One day you will win. Victory will surrender into your feet"

"But I am tired." Anuksha said.

"If it is written in your destiny to see the fulfillment of your dream then you must see the fulfillment. No one can keep you away from this." Anupam said.

Anuksha had a deep sigh. She stared at Anupam. "I always thought that one day I will meet you and you will rescue me from all miseries of life and I would sleep under the roof of your affection." She slowly left her body into warmth of his arms.His arms encircled around her body and she felt the gay warmth deeply for the moment.

— TWENTY EIGHT —

Mr. Putul Dutta had a sudden gaze at Anuksha. There was a kind of wonder and suspicion in his gaze.

"Where did you go in this evening?" Mr. Putul Dutt suddenly asked.

"I went for an evening walk." Anuksha answered gently.

"Don't tell lie." Mr. Putul Dutt said. "I know where did you go? Don't hide it from me. I know you went to meet your old lover."

"Don't say rubbish." Anuksha said.

"You bitch." Mr. Putul Dutt said in a shrill tone. He suddenly took a wooden scale into his hand and hit her. "Tell me what your intention? You both are characterless. You women are always betrayer. You people always play game of polygamy with men. You are not satisfied with one man."

Anuksha was groaning in pain. "Don't beat me. You have no right to beat me.Don't do much. I will inform police." She threatened.

"Don't threat me of police." Mr. Putul Dutt said. "What do you think, I don't know anything? I know everything. I am very open about all these. If you want to marry him then you can marry him. I have no objection. You will get divorce very easily from me. But don't spoil my prestige. Don't sell my prestige in the market. My prestige is not so cheap. I warn you."

"Stop all these." Anuksha shouted almost violently. "You have never reformed yourself and you will never. You are also drunkard and abusive like your elder brother who also never gave me love and happiness who also always tortured me mentally and physically."

"Don't say anything about my late elder brother." Mr. Putul Dutt roared like a tiger. He suddenly raised his fist to hit her face but she resisted.

As Anuksha turned to leave Mr. Putul Dutta he grasped her wrist tightly. He looked up at her face. He laughed almost like a half mad. You are not a caged bird. You are free to fly freely."

Anuksha didn't say anything. She tried to free herself from his grip.

"I know you never wanted to marry my elder brother even me," Mr Putul Dutt said. "You always expected my elder brother's death so that you could marry your old lover. And now you want my death. You are a witch not a devoted wife."

Anuksha had suddenly felt dizziness as if she will lose her conciousness at any moment and fall down on the floor.

Anuksha was silent as Mr. Putul Dutta Continued to rain so many dirty words on her. The vibrations of dirty words tormented her mind.

A few moments later Mr. Putul Dutta's mouth was tired of raining dirty words on her and he stopped his mouth. He freed Anuksha and let her go and he put his hand into pocket and took a Filter cigarette out. He hold the cigarette up side down and lightly patted the tip on the back of his hand then he hold the cigarette in between lips and lit it with a gas lighter.

Anuksha ran into the room. She closed the room from inside and lay on the bed pressing her face into the pillow. The white pillow cover was soaked with tears. She felt very weak and fell into deep asleep after a moment.

After a while Anuksha found herself in a kingdom of dreams. She saw an old man with shortly cut hairs came and sat beside her. The old man wore purely white dress. A golden ring shone brightly on the middle finger of his right hand. He threw a soft look at her running his long fingers on her head very affectionately.

"Don't worry, my child." The old man said. "Very soon you will be free from all torments of life, very soon." He said twice and disappeared.

Then again Anuksha saw herself in a beautiful bridal dress. Her hairs were nicely brushed and waved on her shoulders. Two diamond earrings brightly dazzled in ear lobes. Golden bangles adorned her henna made up hands. She had beautiful make up on her face and a big vermillion mark shone on her forehead. She looked so pretty and charming almost like a new bride sitting on a wonderfully decorated tall chair and waiting for the bride groom to come.

Then suddenly the old man with shortly cut hair and in purely white dress again appeared before her. The old man gently smiled at her. "Look at this wonderfully decorated empty chair beside you." The old man said.

Anuksha slowly turned around and stared at the empty chair beside her.

"That is a very special chair." The old man said smiling.

"Why this is a special chair?" Anuksha asked very innocently.

"Beacause this chair is for a very special man." The old man answered.

"Who is that very special man?" Anuksha asked.

"You guess." The old man answered.A gentle smile shone his face

"What is his name?" Anuksha asked.

"You guess." The old man answered again.

"I can't guess." Anuksha said.

"Anupam," The old man said. He smiled and disappeared again.

"Anupam, the name thrilled Anuksha's whole body. She was so excited as if she had found the most precious gift of life after so many years' worship, as if she had seen the reality of her dream she was carrying so many years in heart.

Then another dream came to her sleep. Anupam walked over her. He wore a beautiful suit. He looked smart and handsome.

Anupam lifted her into air with his two arms. She smiled a fascinating smile. "I am feeling that I am the happiest woman in the world today." She said. The smile was still shinning in her two red lips.

A sudden soft kiss from Anupam's warm lips thrilled her body.

"Anuksha," Anupam whispered. "I am very happy today to see you happy which I always wanted."

Anuksha glanced up at Anupam. Her eyes gleamed with joy.

"I always carried a fear within myself." Anuksha said. "Today you have wiped away that fear from me. You are so kind Anupam, you are so kind." She grabbed him very affectionately with her two arms.

Anupam had no word from his mouth. He slowly put an arm around her.He pressed her passionately.

"I have no one to love me in this world except you." Anuksha said with tearful eyes. "Would you love me forever? Would you give me all happiness of a woman I have missed?"

"Yes." Anupam answered affectionately. I would love you forever. I would get you all happiness of a woman.I will make you the queen of happiness."

— TWENTY NINE —

Next day was a Sunday. Anuksha visited a restaurant along with Anupam and Anuprerana.

Anupam ordered pizza for three of them.Pizza was Anuprerana's favourite.

Anuksha told Anupam about the dream she saw in her sleep previous night.

"What does that dream mean?" Anuksha asked. "Can you analyse that dream?"

Anupam had a gentle look at her face. He had seen a fascination on her face. "I am not a dream analyst." He answered gently. "But I can say that everyone has his or her own way of living and thinking and one day you must get that freedom."

Anuprerana was listening to their conversation minutely.

"Mother," Anuprerana stared at Anuksha. "This short life is a unification of good and bad time. Where there is an end of bad time there is a beginning of good time. I am sure. Your bad time will end one day and your good time will start. What do you say good uncle?" With sudden she asked Anupam.

"You are right, Anuprerana." Anupam answered. "Bad days are not forever. They have no lifes. One day they will surrender to the good days."

The waiter brought pizza on a tray and set on the table.

"Pizza!" Anuprerana uttered widening her eyes.

As the waiter started to move Anupam looked up across him.

"Waiter," Anupam said. Bring three cups of hot coffee.

"Okay." The waiter said politely and went away.

"Do you like coffee?" Anupam asked Anuprerana.

"Yes, Good uncle." Anuprerana quickly answered. "I like coffee very much."

"That is good." Anupam shook his head. "Coffee is not harmful. It energizes you."

"Coffee contains caffeine." Anuprerana said. "It has a stinulating power."

"Yes." Anupam said giving a soft bite into pizza.

Anuksha raised her look at both Anupam and Anuprerana. "Both you can write a thesis on coffee and can obtain a doctorate." She said smiling.

"Yes mother," Anuprerana nodded her head.

Suddenly they burst into laughter together.

As they stepped out of the restaurant they saw four men were carrying an old man covered with white cloth on a bambo bed. The old man was dead. A big crowd of people followed the dead body mourning and chanting God's name. Some of them carried earthen pots in hands.

"The dead man in an old man, Good uncle?" Anuprerana asked. There was little sadness in her voice.

"Yes." Anupam shook his head slowly. "Old age is the time of repentance and last horizon of life. Everything has a limit even a life. Sudden storm arrives from somewhere and free the soul from all torments of life. Death brings salvation to a life."

They hurriedly crossed the street to the other side in a traffic point where there was long queue of vehicle waiting for the green signal to proceed.

"A good news Good uncle," With sudden Anuprerana said staring at Anupam.

Anupam wondered.

"What?" He asked.

"We will spend the whole day in the outside till the evening." Anuprerana said with immense joy and excitement almost like a child. My father had gone to aunt's home. He will stay there for two days."

Anupam had a laugh. "Oh, I see, that is the good news." He laughed again.

"Good uncle." Anuprerana said. "Today is the adventurous day for three of us. Today we three are together, you, mother and I. What a wonderful day today. Is not it good uncle?"

"Yes." Anupam answered smiling.

Anuksha glanced across Anuprerana. "Truly you are a mad girl." She said squeezing her nose.

They boarded a bus towards Ashutosh Chowdhury Avenue where a painting exhibition was going on in an art gallery exhibited by a noted painter of the city.

There was a huge crowd in the gallery. Most of the paintings were oil painting.

The painter in white kurta and pyjama with glasses in eyes was busy narrating about the themes of his paintings to some special guests.

Most of the paintings were costly. Some rich people bought the paintings to enhance the beauty and prestige of their homes and offices.

They walked around the gallery and looked at the paintings. Anuprerana touched some paintings with her fingers and tried to feel the gravity of the paintings. They spent there for about one hour and their eyes felt personified.

They boarded a crowded bus towards Nicco Park. The bus ran in a minimum speed through the zigzag and crowded road of the city. The bus stopped at every stoppage every now and then. Different passengers got out from the long bus and got in to the long bus. Anuprerana enjoyed it very much.

"Nicco Park, Nicco Park". The tall conductor with long beard on the chin almost like a goat shouted as the bus arrived near the Nicco Park.

"Good uncle, we have arrived Nicco Park." Anuprerana said. There was lot of joy in her voice.

They got down of the bus with other passengers. Most of the passengers were visitor to the Nicco Park. Among them were so many children and old man and women.

They spent about two hours there.

A soft melody came from a nearby house as they passed by the old houses of Anglo Indian colony. They peeped through the open window. An Anglo-Indian girl was playing Mozert's in her old piano.

"Wonderful"! Anuksha whispered.

They stopped there for a while and listened to the soft melody. The soft melody created a tide of rare kind of romance in Anupam and Anuksha's hearts. The soft melody took them back to their romantic days of past.

They looked at each other. They felt the sweet sensation very deeply.

"The soft melody has touched my soul and heart." Anuksha said.

"My heart and soul are also very much touched." Anupam said.

When they passed by a big garment shop then the colourful cloths hanging from the wooden rolls in the show room reminded Anuksha about the need to alter the old curtains of home.

"I have to buy some cloths for the curtains of bed room." Anuksha said.

"I was also thinking for some days to tell you about the alteration of the old curtains of the bed room.

Old curtains are faded." Anuprerana swiftly said. "We need to alter them very urgently.They are spoiling the show of the home."

Anuksha bought about twenty metre colourful printed cloths for curtain according Anuprerana's choice.

"You have a good idea about cloth." Anupam said giving a gentle smile at Anuprerana.

They were tired and thirsty. They walked into an open café by the street. They sat at the chairs placed around a round wooden table beneath a big red and white umbrella. They wet their throats with cold drinks.

A calender was hanging in the corner behind the manager's chair. There was a beautiful photograph of two small birds kissing each other with their small beaks. Below the photograph some beautiful words were written— What else is love heavenly for if not to share with others?

The beautiful words gave a beautiful sense of feeling to Anuksha. She couldn't stop herself. She said that whoever wrote those beautiful words was a true worshiper of love.

They spent the whole day enjoying among themselves like a happy small family of father, mother and daughter. Anuksha experienced the true and emotional bond of a happy family.

— THIRTY —

The days passed.

Anupam and Anuksha came much closer day by day. They gradually indulged in intense romance.Their hidden passionate desires burst out they prohibited under the cover of patience and fear for years.

Sometimes cyclonic romance swallowed them like sea waves. They couldn't resist their growing hungers. They freed their growing hungers to taste the freedom. Anuksha forgot for the moment that she was still a devoted wife of someone.

"The life within the tormentation produces a rebellion, indifference, bitterness towards the life itself." Anupam said. "This is not a life you are living. You have to be free. You have to break all barriers and you have to breathe free air."

Anuksha was speechless. She slowly dropped her head over Anupam's arm. Silent tears came out of her eyes soaked his arm.

A deep silence swallowed them gradually like tide.

"Mother, Mother," sudden call of Anuprerana woke up both Anupam and Anuksha from their day dream.

Anuprerana came up the stairs to the roofs.

Anuksha swiftly wiped her tears off.

"What has happened, Anuprerana? Anuksha asked looking up at her.

"Nothing", Anuprerana said calmly. "I have not seen you in the room so."

Anuprerana glanced at Anupam. She softly smiled "Good uncle." She said. "When have you come?"

"Half an hour ago," Anupam answered.

After a while Anuksha got up and told I am going to make tea for all of us. "What do you like to eat with tea, Anuprerana, biscuit or snacks? Your good uncle has brought snacks for you."

"I like to eat snacks while good uncle has brought for me. Anuprerana answered with a delightful mind with a smiling gaze at him.

Anuksha waked down the stairs into the kitchen.

Anuksha came up to the roof a few minutes later with hot tea and snack as Anupam and Anuprerana were busy in story telling.

After they drank tea and ate snacks they come down the stairs. They went to the drawing room. Anupam and Anuprerana sat on the sofa with a chess board and started playing and Anuksha looked on sitting on the sofa beside them.

Anuprerana won two games.

"Good uncle." Anuprerana cheered up. "You can't beat me. I am the unbeatable champion."

Anupam laughed.

"I find happiness and joy in your winning." Anupam said affectionately, "That is my victory. That is the real feeling of victory for me."

"Good uncle." Anuprerana said. There was lot of affection in her tone. "If you were my father then our life would have been so wonderful, Isn't it?"

Anupam nooded his head softly.He raised his eyes at her. He threw a soft look with a strong feeling of emotion at her.

— THIRTY ONE —

When Anuksha looked back to the years she had left she was almost terrified and suffocated.Those were such a days she couldn't forget. They left a deep mark of brutel whip on her soul. She wondered how she digested all the sufferings without a single protest. She had been a patient. She damned god why he had given her strength to endure.

Anuksha hated herself, why she couldn't change herself. She had been the same woman she was before marriage. She was not capable to express her feelings. She was a timid woman. She always hid her true affections towards Anupam.

She married the man she never loved. She couldn't marry the man she always loved. She married a tyrant who can't take Anupam's place in her heart. She still kept an altar separately in heart for Anupam.

Anuksha was not like other women who were brave. She was a timid woman whose dream was dying hungry. Whose heart was torn with pain but still there had been no any change or misery in her love towards Anupam.

If she married Anupam then thing would have been totally different in her life she thought.

Anuksha opened the window. She looked out to the evening street almost in despair.

She thought that God had given her a rare power to face all tyrannies but God hadn't given her the rare power to explode like a bomb against all those.

Then Mr. Putul Dutt arrived home. He was drunk.

"What are you doing?" Mr Putul Dutta asked looking across her.

"Nothing", Anuksha answered reluctantly. "Why do you ask?"

"I thought you are waiting for someone." Putul Dutta answered in a taunting tone. I can't trust you as my wife. You are a love sick woman."

Anuksha didn't say anything. She did not take his saying seriously. She was habituated with this kind of taunting of his husband.

Putul Dutt walked away unsteadily.He muttered something indistinctly. Probably he chid her.

Again Anuksha was left alone with her thought.She tried to find little joy in her thought.

Time was passing very quickly. It was eleven O'clock. She felt tired by her thoughts. She shut the window and went to the bed. She fell into deep asleep. It was summer night. Nigh was short.

Anuksha woke up to the twittering of the sparrows in the morning and another day had begun in her life as usual.

Anuksha looked happy and delightful as she saw Anupam at her home. She forgot all tiredness of the morning.

After Putul Dutt had gone out Anupam and Anuksha sat at the table for breakfast. Anuprerana also joined them in the breakfast.

"I was late to sleep at night so I am late to get up in the morning." Anuprerana said smiling.

"Wouldn't you go to college today?" Anuksha asked.

"No." Anuprerana answered putting a piece of toast into mouth. "Today I will go to collect some important notes from one of my friends."

Then Anuprerana glanced at Anupam. "Would you accompany me, Good uncle?" Anuprerana abruptly asked.

"Where"? Anupam asked.

"To one of my friends' home," Anuprerana answered.

"Okay." Anupam agreed.

Anupam and Anuprerana walked out after breakfast.

"Come soon." Anuksha shouted from behind.

"Okay, mother." Anuprerana waved her hand.

Anuksha stood on the door step and looked on across them untill both disappeared at the end of the street.

"Your mother is timid." Anupam said funnily. "She is not like other modern woman."

"You are right, Good uncle." Anuprerana said. "Whatever my father says she obeys like a loyal servant. She never protests against him. Whenever I see her to be abused in front of me by father then really it pains me too much. You know Good uncle when I was a child then my father always came home late at night. My mother waited for him till the mid night. He was always drunk. He started quarrel with small thing and he started beating my mother. I woke up suddenly. I was so scared then. I pressed my face into the pillow and wept silently. My father had spoilt my mother's beautiful life."

"Don't worry." Anupam said. "God is watching everything from above. He will give the ultimate judgement."

"We are very frank like two friends." Anuprerana said. "We don't hide anything from each other?"

"That is good." Anupam said. "Parents should be frank with their children otherwise so many problems remain unsolved and untold."

They walked on.

"I know your father doesn't like me to see at your home." Anupam said.

"Don't mind that, Good uncle." Anuprerana said. "My father's character is like this. He doesn't like anyone to come to our home from the beginning. You can't change his character. He is the man of unadjustable and jealous mentality."

It was evening when Anupam and Anuprerana returned. They saw Anuksha at the door step waiting for them.

"You are too late." Anuksha said.

"Yes, mother," Anuprerana answered with a tired smile. "I had to write about fifty pages so we are late. Good uncle got bored."

"Not at all," Anupam laughed. Her friend was so nice. She did very good hospitality.And her mother also gave me a sweet company so there was no question of getting bored."

"Now you are both tired and hungry." Anuksha said.

"You both go to the bathroom and wash your hands and mouth. I am arranging meal for you."

"Okay, Mother." Anuksha said.

After meal Anuprerana went to the study room and put her whole concentration into her study because her examination was very near.

Anupam and Anuksha were left alone in the drawing room.

Anupam had a long stare at Anuksha's face with a very kind expression as if he had seen her after long years, as if he had desire to say her that you are mine.

"This can't go on?" Abruptly Anupam said.

"What?" Anuksha asked almost in wonder.

"Aren't you suffocating with this life?" Anupam asked. "Can't you ascape from this life?"

Anuksha was silent.

"You should be brave yourself." Anupam said. "You should stand against all abuses of your husband and this is the only way to escape from the tormenting life."

"You are right Anupam, you are right." Anuksha shook her head. "But I can't."

That evening Putul Dutt arrived home early. He was drunk.

As Putul Dutt saw both Anupam and Anuksha together, he boiled in anger.

Anuksha was little scared.

Putul Dutt looked at them with violent anger as if he wanted to kill them. He hurriedly walked into his room.

"Anuksha, Anuksha." Putul Dutt shouted at Anuksha.

Anuksha walked out of the drawing room and went into husband's room. Putul Dutt shut the door.

"Where is Anuprerana?" Anupam asked suddenly.

"She is studying." Anuksha answered gently.

"What are you doing with that bustard in my absence?" Putul Dutt asked angrily.

"Nothing". Anuksha answered. "We were just talking."

"Do you think I don't know anything?" Putul Dutt said hoarsely. "Both of you always play love in my absence. Neighbours complained me about your illicit affair with that bustard. You have totally spoilt my prestige whatever else left."

Anuksha shut her eyes. She wanted to cry loudly.

"You bitch." Putul Dutt expressed violent anger in his voice.

Then he took a stick and started beating her mercilessly.

"You bitch, untrustful woman." Putul Dutt went on shouting madly "Truly you woman are untrustful."

Anupam heard everything. His heart cried out. He wanted go to defind her but he was helpless. After sometimes he left Anuksha's home with deep mental anguish.

Anuksha lay on the bed. She was groaning in pain. Her heart cried out for Anupam. God how long you will make me suffer in this hell? God, do you want my death too like my mother in penury without love and happiness? She asked looking up at the idol of Lord Siba placed on the altar.

— THIRTY TWO —

It was ten O'Clock in the morning. Anuksha has just finished her breakfast after morning bath. She sat under the ceiling fan and spread her wet hairs over her shoulder to dry. Anuprerana was busy in her study table concentrating on her reference book of economics which she always found very tough.

In the outside the clouds were dropping rains slowly from the sky.

In the meantime with sudden two boys of the colony came running to their home with umbrella over their heads. They brought the shocking news for Anuksha and Anuprerana.

Two boys were breathing heavily. Two boys were little nervous. They were mum for a minute then told that Putul Dutta had been knocked by a speedy car from the back. He has been badly injured on the back of the head. Some local people had rushed him to the nearby Government hospital where he is lying on the bed and struggling with death.

The news had shocked Anuksha. She was almost puzzled. Her mind couldn't find any way what to do and where to go. She was almost nervous and shivering.

Anuprerana controlled herself. She consoled her mother. She phoned to her good uncle Anupam. She told him about the accident and requested him to come immediately.

When Anupam arrived then Anuksha and Anuprerana locked the house and went out in their casual dress. They hired a passing taxi and went to the Government hospital where Putul Dutta was lying on the bed and struggling with death.

They told the driver to drive the taxi fast. But they were not enough lucky to see Putul Dutta alive. He had died before they reached the hospital.

Anuksha was sad. She couldn't make her mind whether she would cry or she would smile. She was almost dumb.

Anuksha felt herself as a very weak woman for the moment.

Anuksha grieved. Again her inner soul said that she married a man who never loved her. Then why should she grieve for him.

When a man dies whether he is liked or disliked we should show last respect to him forgetting all the mistakes or crimes he had done in his life time towards someone. Though he was an abuser but he was hcr husband.

Anuksha sat on the bed beside her hasband Putul Dutta. She looked down on his calms face silently. She had a long look.

"You poor man, you are really unfortunate. You were affluent of only alcohol. In the long twenty years of my married life you had squeezed out all the tears of my eyes. Today not a single drop is left in my eyes to mourn your death. You poor man, you are really unfortunate." Anuksha said in silence.

Anuprerana silently glanced down at her father's calm an unmovable face. She lovelingly touched her father's face for the last time. Tears trickled down her face silently.

Anupam consoled Anuksha. "Everyone has to leave this world." Anupam said. Everyone has to leave this world as soon as he completes his duty on this earth. But ways are different. Someone leaves this world painfully and someone leaves this world peacefully. Difference is here.

Putul Dutta's body was taken to the funeral ground by neighbours.

Anuprerana put fire into the funeral pyre as the only child of her father. Slowly red fire engulfed his body and within an hour his mortal fleshy body was turned into ashes.

Anuksha completed all the rites of her dead husband Putul Dutta nicely according to Hindu religion. After doing all the rites of husband she felt a satisfaction.

— THIRTY THREE —

Anupam always tried to lighten the burden of Anuksha's heart. He was always beside her like a shadow to support her morally and mentally.

Anuksha's memories disturbed her mind every now and then. There was no any sweetness in her memories. There was only bitterness in her memories. In the long years of her married life Putul Dutta only gave her pain. He almost tormented her beautiful life. She tried to forget all her memories though they came every now and then to her mind and disturbed like some immortal parts of life.

Anupam sat beside Anuksha. He gently put his arm around her then he took her head into his bosom very lovingly and very affectionately. She found a great solace.

"Anuksha" Anupam whispered. "I will give you happiness."

A silent glance at Anupam asked so many questions. Are you sure you can give me happiness? Are you sure I will be happy anyday?

"Yes." Anupam whispered again.

Anuksha thought something for a while then she slowly buried her face into soft warmth of his bosom again.

There was a long silence between them. He thought and she also thought. Both were almost unmindful but their thinkings were same and for each other.

"I am feeling a great comfort that I wanted to get long years ago?" Anuksha said. "I want this kind of comfort foreover."

"I promise." Anupam said. He softly kissed on her head.

— THIRTY FOUR —

"I want to say you something if you don't mind mother." Anuprerana said.

"My daughter you can say without any hesitation." Anuksha said. "I won't mind."

"Why don't you marry again?" Anuprerana asked with sudden.

Anuksha was almost surprised and wondered. She was not ready for such a question from Anuprerana. She lost her voice for a second. She laughed. "You have made me laugh my daughter."

"I am serious, mother." Anuprerana said.

"Who is waiting to marry me in this age, my daughter?" Anuksha asked. "I am an old woman now. My days had gone."

"No mother." Anuprerana said soothingly. "You are wrong in your thinking. Your days had not gone. You are still young. Your hairs are black, not grey. Your face is smooth and bright. You have to live so many years. Your days have begun now."

"Who will marry me, my daughter?" Anuksha asked, pulling Anuprerana close with affection.

"There is one person who will marry you." Anuprerana smiled.

"Who?" Anuksha asked. There was enough excitement in her eyes.

"You guess." Anuprerana said. A naughty smile touched her lips.

"I can't guess." Anuksha said.

"Good uncle." Anuprerana said with sudden with full confidence as if a hidden secret came out from the dark.

Anuksha blushed. She slowly lowered her head. But she was delighted mentally.

"Yes mother, yes." Anuprerana said widening her eyes. "I am sure he will marry you and I am sure he will care you and you will be happy forever."

Anuksha blushed.

Then Anuprerana stared into mother's eyes. Tears moistened her eyes. She slowly raised her eyes up and looked at Anuprerana." Are you sure he will marry me?"

"Yes, I am sure he will marry you." Anuprerana answered softly wiping her mother's tears with great affection.

"But there is a big question?" Anuksha said.

"What?"

"A social question", Anuksha answered. Her mind was in a thoughtful mood.

"What social question? Anuprerana asked with little wonder.

"A social barrier," Anuksha answered indifferently.

"Please mother, please." Anuprerana asked in childish tone. "What is the barrier in your marriage with good uncle?"

"A social stigma," Anuksha said. "What people will say if I marry now in this age? I think people will spit on me. They will say that I am a woman of celibacy character, my daughter. People will say that she had a grown up daughter. She should think about her marriage rather she is thinking about her own marriage.

"Remember mother." Anuprerana said strongly. "The minds of the people are very critical. It is very difficult to understand each and everyone's mind. People are jealous by birth. They can't tolerate other's happiness and goodness.And this society has no any principle. This society never praises a good act. So don't bother what people will say, what the society will say. Don't suppress your own happiness and joy fearing the people and the society. Don't keep your soul hungry. Do whatever your soul wants. Mother, look ahead, a beautiful world is waiting for you."

"You are really my great daughter." Anuksha hugged Anuprerana affectionately.

Anuksha couldn't stop her tears. Tears of joy and pain mingled together and burst out of her eyes.

"I am wrong in my opinion about you. Anuksha said. "You are young but your brain is matured enough than other girls of your age. You have taught me a new lesson of life. You have revitalized my dying life. Your mind is great my daughter your mind is great."

"This beautiful life is to live not to ruin." Anuprerana inspired her mother. "And you have to live long with love and joy."

Anuksha had a look at Anuprerana's face with excessive emotion. "I think I am really fortunate. I have got such a great daughter like you." She hugged Anuprerana again.

They wore a shawl of silence for a moment.

Tears were fresh in Anuksha's eyes. Tears made thick layers and streamed down her face.

Anuprerana lovingly wiped mother's tears.

"Truly I was a timid woman until today." Anuksha said. "I never dared to open my mouth. I always suppressed all my joys and happiness. I never allowed them to bloom in my life. I never protested against all the odds done to me by my husband. I tolerated everything silently. I became a tolerating machine. But today you have woken up my sleeping courage. Now I can fight all the injusties done against me. Today I am no more a timid woman. You have made me a brave woman."

"Mother," Anuprerana's voice was gentle. "You have got one life and you enjoy it fully. This life is beautiful and let it bloom beautifully."

"Today I have known that this life is truly beautiful." Anuksha said. Her face was heavy with gentle emotion.

"Then you are ready to marry good uncle?" Anuprerana asked, a splendid smile crossed her face.

Anuksha didn't say anything for a while then she slowly shook her head and blushed.

"Oh my great mother," Anuprerana hugged Anuksha deeply.

"I am feeling, I am the happiest woman in the world. Anuksha said with heavy excitement. "God had given me such a kind hearted daughter like you." She was excited when she thought that she was going to marry Anupam, his love. A rare kind of solace she found on her aching heart.

In the afternoon when Anupam came to their home Anuprerana held his hand and took him to the bed room.

"I have a surprise for you." Anuprerana said. A joyous smile jingled her whole face.

"Surprise," There was wonder in his voice.

"Good uncle." Anuprerana said.

"My mother is ready to marry you. Are you ready?" She asked. "Please don't say no. You have to promise me that you would marry my mother."

Anupam was almost surprised. He was silent. He didn't find word to answer.

"Please good uncle, please." Anuprerana said with childish ego. "Just you tell that you are ready to marry my mother."

Anupam slowly turned around and looked out to the sky. The sky was blue and clear. Then he thought something for a while then he slowly turned his look at Anuprerana. "Yes, I am ready." He said very softly and calmly.

"Hey good uncle," Anuprerana cheered up in full excitement. "Today I feel that I am successful. I am a successful daughter. I have been able to fix two broken hearts. She suddenly climed on the back of Anupam and flooded his face with gentle kisses.

— THIRTY FIVE —

It was month of April. It was spring. Everywhere there was sweet fragrance of romance in the air.

Anupam went to a local priest to discuss about an auspicious day for his and Anuksha's marriage ceremony. The priest chose the 16th April, thrusday as a best day in the month for their marriage.

On the 15th of April in the evening Anupam, Anuksha and Anuprerana went out for shopping for the marriage ceremony. They bought a beautiful and tailored Kurta and Punjabi, a Benarasi saree for Anuksha, jewelleries and some other things for the ceremony only.

Next day they woke up early in the morning. Anuksha was lying on the bed opening her eyes and looking up to the celing. She thought about

Anuksha and Anupam about their marriage and after marriage. She grew up from a young girl to a matured girl for the moment in her thought. She had a marvelous feeling in her mind.

They were ready by ten O'clock. At ten twenty in the morning they went out by the newly bought car of Anupam. They were in joyful mood. Anupam drove down the street across the temple in the out skirt of the city.

Anuprerana sat between Anupam and Anuksha.

Suddenly Anuprerana had a funny idea in her mind. She posed herself as a journalist.

She slowly turned her eyes at Anuksha. She wore a serious gesture in her face as if she was an intelligent journalist and was ready to hit Anupam and mother Anuksha with quations.

"Anuksha," Anuprerana asked with gravity. "What do you think abut your marriage with Anupam?" She asked.

Anuksha smiled shyly. "You naughty girl," She whispered and squeezed her chin.

"Anupam," Anuprerana said turning her look at Anupam. "What do you think about your marriage with Anuksha?" She asked.

"It will be a fruitful marriage." Anupam answered gently.

"My next question to Anuksha," Anuprerana said. "What is your future plan?" She asked.

"Don't be silly my daughter." Anuksha laughed.

Anuprerana looked at Anupam. "My next question to you," Anuprerana said. "What is your future plan?" She asked.

"I have lot of plans." Anupam answered.

"Now my last question to both of you," Anuprerana said with a smile. "How much you are excited about this marriage?" She asked.

"We are too much excited." Anupam answered with a long laugh and Anuksha followed him.

Then with abrupt Anuprerana hugged both mother Anuksha and Anupam with her loving hands in full joy and excitement.

"Good uncle," Anuprerana said. "How much today I am happy you can't imagine. I am feeling a great pleasure and a great coolness in my heart as if someone has sprinkled some cold water on my burning heart. Today I have realized the true feelings of pleasure and joy."

"You are my great daughter." Anuksha said. Then suddenly with excessive emotion and affection she pulled Anuprerana's face towards her and kissed on the cheek.

They had arrived their destination after one and half hour long driving, The Bisnu temple. Anupam parked the car outside the temple. It was about twelve O'clock. There was no much crowd in and around the temple. Most of the people came there for marriage purpose.

Anupam contacted a middle aged priest with long grey hair to perform their marriage ceremony. The priest wore a long red cloth around his body from neck to the knees. He drew long marks of red vermillion on the forehead.

The priest took them to an open place. He lit the holy fire with sandalwood. He sprinkled some perfumes into the fire. The whole surrounding was filled with beautiful fragnance.

Anupam and Anuksha sat before the holy fire. Anupam looked very handsome in his nicely tailored Kurta and pyjama and the wedding crown on the head. A golden ring shone in his middle finger. Anuksha wore the yellow Benarasi saree. Golden ornament around her thin hands made her more beautiful like a new bride and a smartly designed golden necklace around her neck gave extra colour to her beauty.

Anuprerana sat beside her mother Anuksha with a gaiety mind.

The priest started his work. He started to chant mantra in Sanskrit. Every now and then he sprinkled flowers, paddy and kind of holy grasses into holy fire. As the mantra chanting is going on in full swing Anuprerana looked on. She found it very glad and interesting.

Marriage ritual continued for about one hour. Anuksha and Anupam exchanged two specially made golden rings between each other. As Anupam smeared red vermellion over Anuksha's forehead. She had great feeling of holiness in her heart as if her life had been fulfilled.

Then Anupam and Anuksha both stood up and exchanged garlands around their necks and he promised to keep her happy and glad forever keeping the god as witness.

Finally both Anupam and Anuksha touched the feet of the priest then they walked over to the Bishnu idol and touched the brass feet of the Bishnu idol and they took blessings from god Bishnu.

Anushka suddenly remembered her late husband for a moment. Memories dampened her eye for a moment. There was no any sweetness in her memories to remember. There was only bitterness. There was no any true bondage of two souls between them. There was only landslide between two souls.

They came out of the tample and got into the car. Anupam started the car. Anuprerana sat between Anupam and Anuksha. She looked very glad. She looked at both mother Anuksha and Anupam with a great excitement.

Anupam drove the car across the high way. They went to a big hotel of the city. Anupam gave a small party for the occasion. There was no any guest, no any well wishers; only three of them were there.

They created a new world for three of them. It was theirs world.

Anupam ordered about ten items for the dinner.

They took the taste of every item and enjoyed the dinner very nicely.

"Mother," Anuprerana with sudden said getting out of the chair. "Now you enjoy yourselves. Now you should be left alone."

"What are you saying my daughter?" Anuksha asked. "You are the part of my life and my life is for you."

Anuprerana smiled. "Please don't take it any other way. Now you are newly married couple. You should have some kind of privacy. And I don't want to disturb you. Best of luck, you enjoy yourselves. I will see you at home in the evening and you will receive a surprise in the evening." She walked out with a charming smile in her lip looking towards mother.

After spending some private moments closely together Anupam and Anuksha went out for a long drive.

There was no one in between them. They were only two together. They were made for each other. They found the world was very enjoying.

They roamed around the city. They visited the famous and historical places of the city and enjoyed the sweet moments of life together.

In the evening when Anupam and Anuksha returned home they were almost surprised. The door was open. As they walked in a wonderful aroma touched their nostrils.

As they entered the bed room they were more and more astonished. A new big bedsheet was spread on the bed. The bedsheet was beautifully embroidered with two roses in the middle. The bed was nicely decorated with colourful flowers. Everywhere there were only petals of red roses around the bed and costly perfume were spread over the bed sheet. Everywhere there was aroma of romance in the room. "Anuprerana, Anuprerana" Anuksha shouted. But there was no answer. There was no any trace of Anuprerana anywhere around the room. The room had been silent again like before.

As Anuksha turned around to go out of the room suddenly she noticed something written on the wall. She came close to the wall and she was astonished to see the letter written by her daughter to her. She began to read.

"Mother, you are the most loving mother in the world. I wish god bless you thousand blessings. I wish marriage will bring thousand fountains of joy and happiness to your life and your life will be filled with loves and golden smiles and will be bright like the moon of the full moon night forever. Today two hearts and souls reunited into one"

"I had also a past like everyone but difference is there." Anuksha said. "When I peeped into the mirror of my past married life then truly I am terrified. I see nothing there to feel proud. I see nothing merriment there to remember to delight my mind when my mind is sad."

The life went on. Anuksha rediscovered her lost love and happiness within Anupam. She realized the true feelings of happiness and love she always desired. She was very happy and glad. Anupam fulfilled her life with golden rays of joy and happiness he promised to her.

After that her life had been filled with never ending joy and happiness. Now she was a happy woman.

Anuksha was thirsty of love and happiness for whole life but now she had got more then she expected and imagined.